21 Short Tales

FRANZ KAFKA

GENERAL PRESS

Published by

GENERAL PRESS

4805/24, Fourth Floor, Krishna House
Ansari Road, Daryaganj, New Delhi - 110002
Ph : 011-23282971, 45795759
E-mail : generalpressindia@gmail.com

www.generalpress.in

First Edition : 2021

ISBN : 9789354991103

Published by Azeem Ahmad Khan for General Press

BESTSELLING FICTION

- 1984 by George Orwell
  Literature & Fiction, ISBN: 9789380914947
- A Passage to India by E.M. Forster
  Literature & Fiction, ISBN: 9789354990205
- A Room of One's Own by Virginia Woolf
  Literature & Fiction, ISBN: 9789354990281
- A Wrinkle in Time by Madeleine L'Engle
  Literature & Fiction, ISBN: 9789354991066
- Animal Farm by George Orwell
  Literature & Fiction, ISBN: 9789380914701
- Anthem by Ayn Rand
  Literature & Fiction, ISBN: 9789389157079
- As a Man Thinketh by James Allen
  Literature & Fiction, ISBN: 9788180320262
- As I Lay Dying by William Faulkner
  Literature & Fiction, ISBN: 9789390492381
- Demian by Hermann Hesse
  Literature & Fiction, ISBN: 9789387669567
- Lost Horizon by James Hilton
  Literature & Fiction, ISBN: 9789389716313
- Mansarover 1 (Hindi) by Premchand
  Literature & Fiction, ISBN: 9789380914978
- One, None and a Hundred Thousand by Luigi Pirandello
  Literature & Fiction, ISBN: 9789389716337

Search the book by its ISBN

BESTSELLING FICTION

- Siddhartha by Hermann Hesse
  Literature & Fiction, ISBN: 9789380914145
- Tales from Shakespeare by Charles Lamb & Mary Lamb
  Literature & Fiction, ISBN: 9789380914367
- The Mysterious Affair at Styles by Agatha Christie
  Literature & Fiction, ISBN: 9789390492510
- The Plague by Albert Camus
  Literature & Fiction, ISBN: 9788194764892
- The Prophet by Kahlil Gibran
  Literature & Fiction, ISBN: 9789380914022
- The Railway Children by E Nesbit
  Literature & Fiction, ISBN: 9789354990960
- The Sound and the Fury by William Faulkner
  Literature & Fiction, ISBN: 9789390492572
- The Stranger by Albert Camus
  Literature & Fiction, ISBN: 9789390492589
- The Sun Also Rises by Ernest Hemingway
  Literature & Fiction, ISBN: 9789354990984
- Their Eyes Were Watching God by Zora Neale Hurston
  Literature & Fiction, ISBN: 9788194764885
- To the Lighthouse by Virginia Woolf
  Literature & Fiction, ISBN: 9789390492190
- World's Best Short Stories: Volume 1 by Various Authors
  Literature & Fiction, ISBN: 9789390492275

Search the book by its ISBN

Contents

Story 1

BEFORE THE LAW

Before the law sits a gatekeeper. To this gatekeeper comes a man from the country who asks to gain entry into the law. But the gatekeeper says that he cannot grant him entry at the moment. The man thinks about it and then asks if he will be allowed to come in later on. "It is possible," says the gatekeeper, "but not now." At the moment the gate to the law stands open, as always, and the gatekeeper walks to the side, so the man bends over in order to see through the gate into the inside. When the gatekeeper notices that, he laughs and says: "If it tempts you so much, try it in spite of my prohibition. But take note: I am powerful. And I am only the most lowly gatekeeper. But from room to room stand gatekeepers, each more powerful than the other. I can't endure even one glimpse of the third." The man from the country has not expected such difficulties: the law should always be accessible for everyone, he thinks, but as he now looks more closely at the gatekeeper in his fur coat, at his large pointed nose and his long, thin, black Tartar's beard, he decides that it would be better to wait until he gets permission to go inside. The gatekeeper gives him a stool and allows him to sit down at the side in front of the gate. There he sits for days and years. He makes many attempts to be let in, and he wears the gatekeeper out with his requests. The gatekeeper often interrogates him briefly, questioning him about his homeland and many other things, but they are indifferent questions, the kind great men put, and at the end he always tells him once more that he cannot let him inside yet. The man, who has equipped himself with many things for his journey, spends everything, no matter how valuable, to win over the gatekeeper. The latter takes it all but, as he does so, says, "I am taking this only so that you do not think you have failed to do anything." During the many years the man observes the gatekeeper almost continuously. He forgets the other gatekeepers, and this one seems to him the only obstacle for entry into the law. He curses the unlucky circumstance, in the first years thoughtlessly and out loud, later, as he grows old, he still mumbles to himself. He becomes childish and, since in the long years studying the gatekeeper he has come to know the fleas in his fur collar, he even asks the fleas to help him persuade the gatekeeper. Finally his eyesight grows weak, and he does not know whether things are really darker around him or whether his eyes are merely deceiving him. But he recognizes now in the darkness an illumination which breaks inextinguishably out of the gateway to the law. Now he no longer has much time to live. Before his death he gathers in his head all his experiences of the entire time up into one question which he has not yet put to the gatekeeper. He waves to him, since he can no longer lift up his stiffening body.

The gatekeeper has to bend way down to him, for the great difference has changed things to the disadvantage of the man. "What do you still want to know, then?" asks the gatekeeper. "You are insatiable." "Everyone strives after the law," says the man, "so how is that in these many years no one except me has requested entry?"

The gatekeeper sees that the man is already dying and, in order to reach his diminishing sense of hearing, he shouts at him, “Here no one else can gain entry, since this entrance was assigned only to you. I’m going now to close it.

Story 2

AN IMPERIAL MESSAGE

The Emperor—so they say—has sent a message, directly from his death bed, to you alone, his pathetic subject, a tiny shadow which has taken refuge at the furthest distance from the imperial sun. He ordered the herald to kneel down beside his bed and whispered the message in his ear. He thought it was so important that he had the herald speak it back to him. He confirmed the accuracy of verbal message by nodding his head. And in front of the entire crowd of those witnessing his death—all the obstructing walls have been broken down, and all the great ones of his empire are standing in a circle on the broad and high soaring flights of stairs—in front of all of them he dispatched his herald. The messenger started off at once, a powerful, tireless man. Sticking one arm out and then another, he makes his way through the crowd. If he runs into resistance, he points to his breast where there is a sign of the sun. So he moves forwards easily, unlike anyone else. But the crowd is so huge; its dwelling places are infinite. If there were an open field, how he would fly along, and soon you would hear the marvellous pounding of his fist on your door. But instead of that, how futile are all his efforts. He is still forcing his way through the private rooms of the innermost palace. Never will he win his way through. And if he did manage that, nothing would have been achieved. He would have to fight his way down the steps, and, if he managed to do that, nothing would have been achieved. He would have to stride through the courtyards, and after the courtyards through the second palace encircling the first, and, then again, through stairs and courtyards, and then, once again, a palace, and so on for thousands of years. And if he finally burst through the outermost door—but that can never, never happen—the royal capital city, the centre of the world, is still there in front of him, piled high and full of sediment. No one pushes his way through here, certainly not someone with a message from a dead man. But you sit at your window and dream of that message when evening comes.

Story 3

A COUNTRY DOCTOR

I was in great difficulty. An urgent journey was facing me. A seriously ill man was waiting for me in a village ten miles distant. A severe snowstorm filled the space between him and me. I had a carriage—a light one, with large wheels, entirely suitable for our country roads. Wrapped up in furs with the bag of instruments in my hand, I was already standing in the courtyard ready for the journey; but the horse was missing—the horse. My own horse had died the previous night, as a result of over exertion in this icy winter. My servant girl was at that very moment running around the village to see if she could borrow a horse, but it was hopeless—I knew that—and I stood there useless, increasingly covered with snow, becoming all the time more immobile. The girl appeared at the gate, alone. She was swinging the lantern. Of course, who is now going to lend her his horse for such a journey? I walked once again across the courtyard. I couldn't see what to do. Distracted and tormented, I kicked my foot against the cracked door of the pig sty which had not been used for years. The door opened and banged to and fro on its hinges. A warmth and smell as if from horses came out. A dim stall lantern on a rope swayed inside. A man huddled down in the stall below showed his open blue eyed face. "Shall I hitch up?" he asked, crawling out on all fours. I didn't know what to say and bent down to see what was still in the stall. The servant girl stood beside me. "One doesn't know the sorts of things one has stored in one's own house," she said, and we both laughed. "Hey, Brother, hey Sister," the groom cried out, and two horses, powerful animals with strong flanks, shoved their way one behind the other, legs close to the bodies, lowering their well formed heads like camels, and getting through the door space, which they completely filled, only through the powerful movements of their rumps. But right away they stood up straight, long legged, with thick steaming bodies. "Help him," I said, and the girl obediently hurried to hand the wagon harness to the groom. But as soon as she was beside him, the groom puts his arms around her and pushes his face against hers. She screams out and runs over to me. On the girl's cheek were red marks from two rows of teeth. "You brute," I cry out in fury, "do you want the whip?" But I immediately remember that he is a stranger, that I don't know where he comes from, and that he's helping me out of his own free will, when everyone else is refusing to. As if he knows what I was thinking, he takes no offence at my threat, but turns around to me once more, still busy with the horses. Then he says, "Climb in," and, in fact, everything is ready. I notice that I have never before travelled with such a beautiful team of horses, and I climb in happily. "But I'll take the reins. You don't know the way," I say. "Of course," he says; "I'm not going with you.

I'm staying with Rosa." "No," screams Rosa and runs into the house, with an accurate premonition of the inevitability of her fate. I hear the door chain rattling as she sets it in place. I hear the lock click. I see how in addition she runs down the corridor and through the rooms putting out all the lights in order to make herself impossible to find. “You’re coming with me,” I say to the groom, “or I’ll give up the journey, no matter how urgent it is. It’s not my intention to give you the girl as the price of the trip.” “Giddy up,” he says and claps his hands. The carriage is torn away, like a piece of wood in a current. I still hear how the door of my house is breaking down and splitting apart under the groom’s onslaught, and then my eyes and ears are filled with a roaring sound which overwhelms all my senses at once. But only for a moment. Then I am already there, as if the farm yard of my invalid opens up immediately in front of my courtyard gate. The horses stand quietly. The snowfall has stopped, moonlight all around. The sick man’s parents rush out of the house, his sister behind them. They almost lift me out of the carriage. I get nothing from their confused talking. In the sick room one can hardly breathe the air. The neglected cooking stove is smoking. I want to push open the window, but first I’ll look at the sick man. Thin, without fever, not cold, not warm, with empty eyes, without a shirt, the young man under the stuffed quilt heaves himself up, hangs around my throat, and whispers in my ear, “Doctor, let me die.” I look around. No one has heard. The parents stand silently, leaning forward, and wait for my opinion. The sister has brought a stool for my handbag. I open the bag and look among my instruments. The young man constantly gropes at me from the bed to remind me of his request. I take some tweezers, test them in the candle light, and put them back. “Yes,” I think blasphemously, “in such cases the gods do help. They send the missing horse, even add a second one because it’s urgent, and even throw in a groom as a bonus.” Now for the first time I think once more of Rosa. What am I doing? How am I saving her? How do I pull her out from under this groom, ten miles away from her, with uncontrollable horses in the front of my carriage? These horses, who have somehow loosened their straps, are pushing open the window from outside, I don't know how. Each one is sticking its head through a window and, unmoved by the crying of the family, is observing the invalid. "I'll go back right away," I think, as if the horses were ordering me to journey back, but I allow the sister, who thinks I am in a daze because of the heat, to take off my fur coat. A glass of rum is prepared for me. The old man claps me on the shoulder; the sacrifice of his treasure justifies this familiarity. I shake my head. In the narrow circle of the old man's thinking I was not well; that's the only reason I refuse to drink.

The mother stands by the bed and entices me over. I follow and, as a horse neighs loudly at the ceiling, lay my head on the young man's chest, which trembles under my wet beard. That confirms what I know: the young man is healthy. His circulation is a little off, saturated with coffee by his caring mother, but he's healthy and best pushed out of bed with a shove. I'm no improver of the world and let him live there. I am employed by the district and do my duty to the full, right to the point where it's almost too much. Badly paid, but I'm generous and ready to help the poor. I still have to look after Rosa, and then the young man may have his way, and I want to die too. What am I doing here in this endless winter! My horse is dead, and there is no one in the village who'll lend me his. I have to drag my team out of the pig sty. If they hadn't happened to be horses, I'd have had to travel with pigs. That's the way it is. And I nod to the family. They know nothing about it, and if they did know, they wouldn't believe it. Incidentally, it's easy to write prescriptions, but difficult to come to an understanding with people. Now, at this point my visit might have come to an end—they have once more called for my help unnecessarily. I'm used to that. With the help of my night bell the entire region torments me, but that this time I had to sacrifice Rosa as well, this beautiful girl, who lives in my house all year long and whom I scarcely notice—this sacrifice is too great, and I must somehow in my own head subtly rationalize it away for the moment, in order not to let loose at this family who cannot, even with their best will, give me Rosa back again. But as I am closing up by hand bag and calling for my fur coat, the family is standing together, the father sniffing the glass of rum in his hand, the mother, probably disappointed in me—what more do these people expect?—tearfully biting her lips, and the sister flapping a very bloody hand towel, I am somehow ready, in the circumstances, to concede that the young man is perhaps nonetheless sick. I go to him. He smiles up at me, as if I was bringing him the most nourishing kind of soup—ah, now both horses are whinnying, the noise is probably supposed to come from higher regions in order to illuminate my examination—and now I find out that, yes indeed, the young man is ill. On his right side, in the region of the hip, a wound the size of the palm of one's hand has opened up. Rose coloured, in many different shadings, dark in the depths, brighter on the edges, delicately grained, with uneven patches of blood, open to the light like a mine. That's what it looks like from a distance. Close up a complication is apparent. Who can look at that without whistling softly? Worms, as thick and long as my little finger, themselves rose coloured and also spattered with blood, are wriggling their white bodies with many limbs from their stronghold in the inner of the wound towards the light. Poor young man, there's no helping you.

I have found out your great wound. You are dying from this flower on your side. The family is happy; they see me doing something. The sister says that to the mother, the mother tells the father, the father tells a few guests who are coming in on tip toe through the moonlight of the open door, balancing themselves with outstretched arms. "Will you save me?" whispers the young man, sobbing, quite blinded by the life inside his wound. That's how people are in my region. Always demanding the impossible from the doctor. They have lost the old faith. The priest sits at home and tears his religious robes to pieces, one after the other. But the doctor is supposed to achieve everything with his delicate surgeon's hand. Well, it's what they like to think. I have not offered myself. If they use me for sacred purposes, I let that happen to me as well. What more do I want, an old country doctor, robbed of my servant girl! And they come, the families and the village elders, and take my clothes off. A choir of school children with the teacher at the head stands in front of the house and sings an extremely simple melody with the words

> *Take his clothes off, then he'll heal,*
> *and if he doesn't cure, then kill him.*
> *It's only a doctor; it's only a doctor.*

Then I am stripped of my clothes and, with my fingers in my beard and my head tilted to one side, I look at the people quietly. I am completely calm and clear about everything and stay that way, too, although it is not helping me at all, for they are now taking me by the head and feet and dragging me into bed. They lay me against the wall on the side of wound. Then they all go out of the room. The door is shut. The singing stops. Clouds move in front of the moon. The bedclothes lie warmly around me. In the open space of the windows the horses' heads sway like shadows. "Do you know," I hear someone saying in my ear, "my confidence in you is very small. You were shaken out from somewhere. You don't come on your own feet. Instead of helping, you give me less room on my deathbed. The best thing would be if I scratch your eyes out." "Right," I say, "it's a disgrace. But now I'm a doctor. What am I supposed to do? Believe me, things are not easy for me either." "Should I be satisfied with this excuse? Alas, I'll probably have to be. I always have to make do. I came into the world with a beautiful wound; that was all I was furnished with." "Young friend," I say, "your mistake is that you have no perspective. I've already been in all the sick rooms, far and wide, and I tell you your wound is not so bad. Made in a tight corner with two blows from an axe. Many people offer their side and hardly hear the axe in the forest, to say nothing of the fact that it's coming closer to them." "Is that really so, or are you deceiving me in my fever?" "It is truly so. Take the word of honour of a medical doctor." He took my word and grew still.

But now it was time to think about my escape. The horses were still standing loyally in place. Clothes, fur coat, and bag were quickly snatched up. I didn't want to delay by getting dressed; if the horses rushed as they had on the journey out, I should, in fact, be springing out of that bed into my own, as it were. One horse obediently pulled back from the window. I threw the bundle into the carriage. The fur coat flew too far and was caught on a hook by only one arm. Good enough. I swung myself up onto the horse. The reins dragging loosely, one horse barely harnessed to the other, the carriage-swaying behind, last of all the fur coat in the snow. "Giddy up," I said, but there was no giddying up about it. We dragged through the snowy desert like old men; for a long time the fresh but inaccurate singing of the children resounded behind us:

Enjoy yourselves, you patients.
The doctor's laid in bed with you.

I'll never come home at this rate. My flourishing practice is lost. A successor is robbing me, but to no avail, for he cannot replace me. In my house the disgusting groom is wreaking havoc. Rosa is his victim. I will not think it through. Naked, abandoned to the frost of this unhappy age, with an earthly carriage and unearthly horses, I drive around by myself, an old man. My fur coat hangs behind the wagon, but I cannot reach it, and no one from the nimble rabble of patients lifts a finger. Betrayed! Betrayed! Once one responds to a false alarm on the night bell, there's no making it good again—not ever.

Story 4

JACKALS AND ARABS

We were camping in the oasis. My companions were asleep. An Arab, tall and dressed in white, went past me. He had been tending to his camels and was going to his sleeping place.

I threw myself on my back into the grass. I wanted to sleep. I couldn't. The howling of a jackal in the distance—I sat up straight again. And what had been so far away was suddenly close by. A swarming pack of jackals around me, their eyes flashing dull gold and going out, slender bodies moving in a quick, coordinated manner, as if responding to a whip.

One of them came from behind, pushed himself under my arm, right against me, as if it needed my warmth, then stepped in front of me and spoke, almost eye to eye with me.

"I'm the oldest jackal for miles around. I'm happy I'm still able to welcome you here. I had already almost given up hope, for we've been waiting for you an infinitely long time. My mother waited, and her mother, and all her mothers, right back to the mother of all jackals. Believe me!"

"That surprises me," I said, forgetting to light the pile of wood which lay ready to keep the jackals away with its smoke, "I'm very surprised to hear that. I've come from the high north merely by chance and am in the middle of a short trip. What do you jackals want then?"

As if encouraged by this conversation, which was perhaps too friendly, they drew their circle more closely around me, all panting and snarling.

"We know," the oldest began, "that you come from the north. Our hope rests on that very point. In the north there is a way of understanding things which one cannot find here among the Arabs. You know, from their cool arrogance one cannot strike a spark of common sense. They kill animals to eat them, and they disregard rotting carcasses."

"Don't speak so loud," I said. "There are Arabs sleeping close by."

"You really are a stranger," said the jackal. "Otherwise you would know that throughout the history of the world a jackal has never yet feared an Arab. Should we fear them? Is it not misfortune enough that we have been cast out among such people?"

"Maybe—that could be," I said. "I'm not up to judging things which are so far removed from me. It seems to be a very old conflict—it's probably in the blood and so perhaps will only end with blood."

"You are very clever" said the old jackal, and they all panted even more quickly, their lungs breathing rapidly, although they were standing still. A bitter smell streamed out of their open jaws—at times I could tolerate it only by clenching my teeth. "You are very clever. What you said corresponds to our ancient doctrine. So we take their blood, and the quarrel is over."

"Oh," I said, more sharply than I intended, "they'll defend themselves. They'll shoot you down in droves with their guns.

"You do not understand us," he said, "a characteristic of human beings which has not disappeared, not even in the high north. We are not going to kill them. The Nile would not have enough water to wash us clean. The very sight of their living bodies makes us run away immediately into cleaner air, into the desert, which, for that very reason, is our home."

All the jackals surrounding us—and in the meantime many more had come up from a distance—lowered their heads between the front legs and cleaned them with their paws. It was as if they wanted to conceal an aversion which was so terrible, that I would have much preferred to take a big jump and escape beyond their circle.

"So what do you intend to do," I asked. I wanted to stand up, but I couldn't. Two young animals were holding me firmly from behind with their jaws biting my jacket and shirt. I had to remain sitting. "They are holding your train," said the old jackal seriously, by way of explanation, "a mark of respect." "They should let me go," I cried out, turning back and forth between the old one and the young ones. "Of course, they will," said the old one, "if that's what you want. But it will take a little while, for, as is our habit, they have dug their teeth in deep and must first let their jaws open gradually. Meanwhile, listen to our request." "Your conduct has not made me particularly receptive to it," I said. "Don't make us pay for our clumsiness," he said, and now for the first time he brought the plaintive tone of his natural voice to his assistance. "We are poor animals—all we have is our teeth. For everything we want to do—good and bad—the only thing available to us is our teeth." "So what do you want?" I asked, only slightly reassured.

"Sir," he cried out, and all the jackals howled. To me it sounded very remotely like a melody. "Sir, you should end the quarrel which divides the world in two. Our ancestors described a man like you as the one who will do it. We must be free of the Arabs—with air we can breathe, a view of the horizon around us clear of Arabs, no cries of pain from a sheep which an Arab has knifed, and every animal should die peacefully and be left undisturbed for us to drain it empty and clean it right down to the bones. Cleanliness—that's what we want— nothing but cleanliness." Now they were all crying and sobbing. "How can you bear it in this world, you noble heart and sweet entrails? Dirt is their white; dirt is their black; their beards are horrible; looking at the corner of their eyes makes one spit; and if they lift their arms, hell opens up in their arm pits. And that's why, sir, that's why, my dear sir, with the help of your all capable hands you must use these scissors to slit right through their throats". He jerked his head, and in response a jackal came up carrying on its canine tooth a small pair of sewing scissors covered with old rust.

"So finally the scissors—it's time to stop!" cried the Arab leader of our caravan, who had crept up on us from downwind. Now he swung his gigantic whip.

The jackals all fled quickly, but still remained at some distance huddled closely together, many animals so close and stiff that it looked as if they were in a narrow pen with jack o' lanterns flying around them.

"So, you too, sir, have seen and heard this spectacle," said the Arab, laughing as cheerfully as the reticence of his race permitted. "So you know what the animals want," I asked. "Of course, sir," he said. "That's common knowledge—as long as there are Arabs, these scissors will wander with us through the deserts until the end of days. Every European is offered them for the great work; every European is exactly the one they think qualified to do it. These animals have an absurd hope. They're idiots, real idiots. That's why we're fond of them. They are our dogs, finer than the ones you have. Now, watch this. In the night a camel died. I have had it brought here."

Four bearers came and threw the heavy carcass right in front of us. No sooner was it lying there than the jackals raised their voices. Every one of them crept forward, its body scraping the ground, as if drawn by an irresistible rope. They had forgotten the Arabs, forgotten their hatred. The presence of a powerfully stinking dead body wiped out everything and enchanted them. One of them was already hanging at the camel's throat and with its first bite had found the artery. Like a small angry pump which—with a determination matched only by its hopelessness—seeks to put out an overpowering fire, every muscle of its body pulled and twitched in its place. Then right away all them were lying there on the corpse working in the same way, piled up like a mountain.

Then the leader cracked his sharp whip powerfully all around above them. They raised their heads, half fainting in their intoxicated state, looked at the Arab standing in front of them, started to feel the whip now hitting their muzzles, jumped away, and ran back a distance. But the camel's blood was already lying there in pools, stinking to heaven, and the body was torn wide open in several places. They could not resist. They were there again. The leader once more raised his whip. I grabbed his arm. "Sir, you are right," he said. "We'll leave them to their calling. Besides, it's time to break camp. You've seen them. Wonderful creatures, aren't they? and how they hate us!"

Story 5

A HUNGER ARTIST

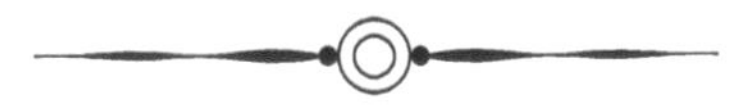

In the last decades interest in hunger artists has declined considerably. Whereas in earlier days there was good money to be earned putting on major productions of this sort under one's own management, nowadays that is totally impossible. Those were different times. Back then the hunger artist captured the attention of the entire city. From day to day while the fasting lasted, participation increased. Everyone wanted to see the hunger artist at least daily. During the final days there were people with subscription tickets who sat all day in front of the small barred cage. And there were even viewing hours at night, their impact heightened by torchlight. On fine days the cage was dragged out into the open air, and then the hunger artist was put on display particularly for the children. While for grown-ups the hunger artist was often merely a joke, something they participated in because it was fashionable, the children looked on amazed, their mouths open, holding each other's hands for safety, as he sat there on scattered straw—spurning a chair—in a black tights, looking pale, with his ribs sticking out prominently, sometimes nodding politely, answering questions with a forced smile, even sticking his arm out through the bars to let people feel how emaciated he was, but then completely sinking back into himself, so that he paid no attention to anything, not even to what was so important to him, the striking of the clock, which was the single furnishing in the cage, merely looking out in front of him with his eyes almost shut and now and then sipping from a tiny glass of water to moisten his lips.

Apart from the changing groups of spectators there were also constant observers chosen by the public—strangely enough they were usually butchers—who, always three at a time, were given the task of observing the hunger artist day and night, so that he didn't get something to eat in some secret manner. It was, however, merely a formality, introduced to reassure the masses, for those who understood knew well enough that during the period of fasting the hunger artist would never, under any circumstances, have eaten the slightest thing, not even if compelled by force. The honour of his art forbade it. Naturally, none of the watchers understood that. Sometimes there were nightly groups of watchers who carried out their vigil very laxly, deliberately sitting together in a distant corner and putting all their attention into playing cards there, clearly intending to allow the hunger artist a small refreshment, which, according to their way of thinking, he could get from some secret supplies. Nothing was more excruciating to the hunger artist than such watchers. They depressed him. They made his fasting terribly difficult.

Sometimes he overcame his weakness and sang during the time they were observing, for as long as he could keep it up, to show people how unjust their suspicions about him were. But that was little help. For then they just wondered among themselves about his skill at being able to eat even while singing. He much preferred the observers who sat down right against the bars and, not satisfied with the dim backlighting of the room, illuminated him with electric flashlights. The glaring light didn't bother him in the slightest. Generally he couldn't sleep at all, and he could always doze under any lighting and at any hour, even in an overcrowded, noisy auditorium. With such observers, he was very happily prepared to spend the entire night without sleeping. He was very pleased to joke with them, to recount stories from his nomadic life and then, in turn, to listen their stories—doing everything just to keep them awake, so that he could keep showing them once again that he had nothing to eat in his cage and that he was fasting as none of them could.

He was happiest, however, when morning came and a lavish breakfast was brought for them at his own expense, on which they hurled themselves with the appetite of healthy men after a hard night's work without sleep. True, there were still people who wanted to see in this breakfast an unfair means of influencing the observers, but that was going too far, and if they were asked whether they wanted to undertake the observers' night shift for its own sake, without the breakfast, they excused themselves. But nonetheless they stood by their suspicions.

However, it was, in general, part of fasting that these doubts were inextricably associated with it. For, in fact, no one was in a position to spend time watching the hunger artist every day and night, so no one could know, on the basis of his own observation, whether this was a case of truly uninterrupted, flawless fasting. The hunger artist himself was the only one who could know that and, at the same time, the only spectator capable of being completely satisfied with his own fasting. But the reason he was never satisfied was something different. Perhaps it was not fasting at all which made him so very emaciated that many people, to their own regret, had to stay away from his performance, because they couldn't bear to look at him. For he was also so skeletal out of dissatisfaction with himself, because he alone knew something that even initiates didn't know—how easy it was too fast. It was the easiest thing in the world. About this he did not remain silent, but people did not believe him. At best they thought he was being modest. Most of them, however, believed he was a publicity seeker or a total swindler, for whom, at all events, fasting was easy, because he understood how to make it easy, and then had the nerve to half admit it. He had to accept all that. Over the years he had become accustomed to it. But this dissatisfaction kept gnawing at his insides all the time and never yet—and this one had to say to his credit—had he left the cage of his own free will after any period of fasting.

The impresario had set the maximum length of time for the fast at forty days—he would never allow the fasting go on beyond that point, not even in the cosmopolitan cities. And, in fact, he had a good reason. Experience had shown that for about forty days one could increasingly whip up a city's interest by gradually increasing advertising, but that then the people turned away—one could demonstrate a significant decline in popularity. In this respect, there were, of course, small differences among different towns and among different countries, but as a rule it was true that forty days was the maximum length of time.

So then on the fortieth day the door of the cage—which was covered with flowers—was opened, an enthusiastic audience filled the amphitheatre, a military band played, two doctors entered the cage, in order to take the necessary measurements of the hunger artist, the results were announced to the auditorium through a megaphone, and finally two young ladies arrived, happy about the fact that they were the ones who had just been selected by lot, seeking to lead the hunger artist down a couple of steps out of the cage, where on a small table a carefully chosen hospital meal was laid out. And at this moment the hunger artist always fought back.

Of course, he still freely laid his bony arms in the helpful outstretched hands of the ladies bending over him, but he did not want to stand up. Why stop right now after forty days? He could have kept going for even longer, for an unlimited length of time. Why stop right now, when he was in his best form, indeed, not yet even in his best fasting form? Why did people want to rob him of the fame of fasting longer, not just so that he could become the greatest hunger artist of all time, which he probably was already, but also so that he could surpass himself in some unimaginable way, for he felt there were no limits to his capacity for fasting. Why did this crowd, which pretended to admire him so much, have so little patience with him? If he kept going and kept fasting longer, why would they not tolerate it? Then, too, he was tired and felt good sitting in the straw. Now he was supposed to stand up straight and tall and go to eat, something which, when he just imagined it, made him feel nauseous right away. With great difficulty he repressed mentioning this only out of consideration for the women. And he looked up into the eyes of these women, apparently so friendly but in reality so cruel, and shook his excessively heavy head on his feeble neck.

But then happened what always happened.

The impresario came and in silence—the music made talking impossible—raised his arms over the hunger artist, as if inviting heaven to look upon its work here on the straw, this unfortunate martyr, something the hunger artist certainly was, only in a completely different sense, then grabbed the hunger artist around his thin waist, in the process wanting with his exaggerated caution to make people believe that here he had to deal with something fragile, and handed him over—not without secretly shaking him a little, so that the hunger artist's legs and upper body swung back and forth uncontrollably—to the women, who had in the meantime turned as pale as death. At this point, the hunger artist endured everything. His head lay on his chest—it was as if it had inexplicably rolled around and just stopped there—his body was arched back, his legs, in an impulse of self-preservation, pressed themselves together at the knees, but scraped the ground, as if they were not really on the floor but were looking for the real ground, and the entire weight of his body, admittedly very small, lay against one of the women, who appealed for help with flustered breath, for she had not imagined her post of honour would be like this, and then stretched her neck as far as possible, to keep her face from the least contact with the hunger artist, but then, when she couldn't manage this and her more fortunate companion didn't come to her assistance but trembled and remained content to hold in front of her the hunger artist's hand, that small bundle of knuckles, she broke into tears, to the delighted laughter of the auditorium, and had to be relieved by an attendant who had been standing ready for some time. Then came the meal. The impresario put a little food into mouth of the hunger artist, now half unconscious, as if fainting, and kept up a cheerful patter designed to divert attention away from the hunger artist's condition. Then a toast was proposed to the public, which was supposedly whispered to the impresario by the hunger artist, the orchestra confirmed everything with a great fanfare, people dispersed, and no one had the right to be dissatisfied with the event, no one except the hunger artist—he was always the only one.

He lived this way, taking small regular breaks, for many years, apparently in the spotlight, honoured by the world, but for all that his mood was usually gloomy, and it kept growing gloomier all the time, because no one understood how to take him seriously. But how was he to find consolation? What was there left for him to wish for? And if a good natured man who felt sorry for him ever wanted to explain to him that his sadness probably came from his fasting, then it could happen that the hunger artist responded with an outburst of rage and began to shake the bars like an animal, frightening everyone. But the impresario had a way of punishing moments like this, something he was happy to use. He would make an apology for the hunger artist to the assembled public, conceding that the irritability had been provoked only by his fasting, something quite intelligible to well fed people and capable of excusing the behaviour of the hunger artist without further explanation.

From there he would move on to speak about the equally hard to understand claim of the hunger artist that he could go on fasting for much longer than he was doing. He would praise the lofty striving, the good will, and the great self-denial no doubt contained in this claim, but then would try to contradict it simply by producing photographs, which were also on sale, for in the pictures one could see the hunger artist on the fortieth day of his fast, in bed, almost dead from exhaustion. Although the hunger artist was very familiar with this perversion of the truth, it always strained his nerves again and was too much for him. What was a result of the premature ending of the fast people were now proposing as its cause! It was impossible to fight against this lack of understanding, against this world of misunderstanding. In good faith he always listened eagerly to the impresario at the bars of his cage, but each time, once the photographs came out, he would let go of the bars and, with a sigh, sink back into the straw, and a reassured public could come up again and view him.

When those who had witnessed such scenes thought back on them a few years later, often they were unable to understand themselves. For in the meantime that change mentioned above had set it. It happened almost immediately. There may have been more profound reasons for it, but who bothered to discover what they were? At any rate, one day the pampered hunger artist saw himself abandoned by the crowd of pleasure seekers, who preferred to stream to other attractions. The impresario chased around half of Europe one more time with him, to see whether he could still re-discover the old interest here and there. It was all futile. It was as if a secret agreement against the fasting performances had developed everywhere. Naturally, it couldn't really have happened all at once, and people later remembered some things which in the days of intoxicating success they hadn't paid sufficient attention to, some inadequately suppressed indications, but now it was too late to do anything to counter them. Of course, it was certain that the popularity of fasting would return once more someday, but for those now alive that was no consolation. What was the hunger artist to do now? A man whom thousands of people had cheered on could not display himself in show booths at small fun fairs. The hunger artist was not only too old to take up a different profession, but was fanatically devoted to fasting more than anything else. So he said farewell to the impresario, an incomparable companion on his life's road, and let himself be hired by a large circus. In order to spare his own feelings, he didn't even look at the terms of his contract at all.

A large circus with its huge number of men, animals, and gimmicks, which are constantly being let go and replenished, can use anyone at any time, even a hunger artist, provided, of course, his demands are modest. Moreover, in this particular case it was not only the hunger artist himself who was engaged, but also his old and famous name.

In fact, given the characteristic nature of his art, which was not diminished by his advancing age, one could never claim that a worn out artist, who no longer stood at the pinnacle of his ability, wanted to escape to a quiet position in the circus. On the contrary, the hunger artist declared that he could fast just as well as in earlier times—something that was entirely credible. Indeed, he even affirmed that if people would let him do what he wanted—

and he was promised this without further ado—he would really now legitimately amaze the world for the first time, an assertion which, however, given the mood of the time, which the hunger artist in his enthusiasm easily overlooked, only brought smiles from the experts.

However, basically the hunger artist had not forgotten his sense of the way things really were, and he took it as self evident that people would not set him and his cage up as the star attraction somewhere in the middle of the arena, but would move him outside in some other readily accessible spot near the animal stalls. Huge brightly painted signs surrounded the cage and announced what there was to look at there. During the intervals in the main performance, when the general public pushed out towards the menagerie in order to see the animals, they could hardly avoid moving past the hunger artist and stopping there a moment. They would perhaps have remained with him longer, if those pushing up behind them in the narrow passage way, who did not understand this pause on the way to the animal stalls they wanted to see, had not made a longer peaceful observation impossible. This was also the reason why the hunger artist began to tremble at these visiting hours, which he naturally used to long for as the main purpose of his life. In the early days he could hardly wait for the pauses in the performances. He had looked forward with delight to the crowd pouring around him, until he became convinced only too quickly—and even the most stubborn, almost deliberate self-deception could not hold out against the experience—that, judging by their intentions, most of these people were, again and again without exception, only visiting the menagerie. And this view from a distance still remained his most beautiful moment. For when they had come right up to him, he immediately got an earful from the shouting of the two steadily increasing groups, the ones who wanted to take their time looking at the hunger artist, not with any understanding but on a whim or from mere defiance—for him these ones were soon the more painful—and a second group of people whose only demand was to go straight to the animal stalls.

Once the large crowds had passed, the late comers would arrive, and although there was nothing preventing these people any more from sticking around for as long as they wanted, they rushed past with long strides, almost without a sideways glance, to get to the animals in time.

And it was an all-too-rare stroke of luck when the father of a family came by with his children, pointed his finger at the hunger artist, gave a detailed explanation about what was going on here, and talked of earlier years, when he had been present at similar but incomparably more magnificent performances, and then the children, because they had been inadequately prepared at school and in life, always stood around still uncomprehendingly. What was fasting to them? But nonetheless the brightness of the look in their searching eyes revealed something of new and more gracious times coming. Perhaps, the hunger artist said to himself sometimes, everything would be a little better if his location were not quite so near the animal stalls. That way it would be easy for people to make their choice, to say nothing of the fact that he was very upset and constantly depressed by the stink from the stalls, the animals' commotion at night, the pieces of raw meat dragged past him for the carnivorous beasts, and the roars at feeding time. But he did not dare to approach the administration about it. In any case, he had the animals to thank for the crowds of visitors among whom, here and there, there could be one destined for him. And who knew where they would hide him if he wished to remind them of his existence and, along with that, of the fact that, strictly speaking, he was only an obstacle on the way to the menagerie.

A small obstacle, at any rate, a constantly diminishing obstacle. People got used to the strange notion that in these times they would want to pay attention to a hunger artist, and with this habitual awareness the judgment on him was pronounced. He might fast as well as he could—and he did—but nothing could save him anymore. People went straight past him. Try to explain the art of fasting to anyone! If someone doesn't feel it, then he cannot be made to understand it. The beautiful signs became dirty and illegible. People tore them down, and no one thought of replacing them. The small table with the number of days the fasting had lasted, which early on had been carefully renewed every day, remained unchanged for a long time, for after the first weeks the staff grew tired of even this small task. And so the hunger artist kept fasting on and on, as he once had dreamed about in earlier times, and he had no difficulty succeeding in achieving what he had predicted back then, but no one was counting the days—no one, not even the hunger artist himself, knew how great his achievement was by this point, and his heart grew heavy. And when once in a while a person strolling past stood there making fun of the old number and talking of a swindle, that was in a sense the stupidest lie which indifference and innate maliciousness could invent, for the hunger artist was not being deceptive—he was working honestly—but the world was cheating him of his reward.

Many days went by once more, and this, too, came to an end.

Finally the cage caught the attention of a supervisor, and he asked the attendant why they had left this perfectly useful cage standing here unused with rotting straw inside. Nobody knew, until one man, with the help of the table with the number on it, remembered the hunger artist. They pushed the straw around with a pole and found the hunger artist in there. "Are you still fasting?" the supervisor asked. "When are you finally going to stop?"

"Forgive me everything," whispered the hunger artist. Only the supervisor, who was pressing his ear up against the cage, understood him. "Certainly," said the supervisor, tapping his forehead with his finger in order to indicate to the spectators the state the hunger artist was in, "we forgive you." "I always wanted you to admire my fasting," said the hunger artist. "But we do admire it," said the supervisor obligingly. "But you shouldn't admire it," said the hunger artist. "Well then, we don't admire it," said the supervisor, "but why shouldn't we admire it?" "Because I had to fast. I can't do anything else," said the hunger artist. "Just look at you," said the supervisor, "why can't you do anything else?" "Because," said the hunger artist, lifting his head a little and, with his lips pursed as if for a kiss, speaking right into the supervisor's ear so that he wouldn't miss anything, "because I couldn't find a food which I enjoyed. If had found that, believe me, I would not have made a spectacle of myself and would have eaten to my heart's content, like you and everyone else." Those were his last words, but in his failing eyes there was the firm, if no longer proud, conviction that he was continuing to fast.

"All right, tidy this up now," said the supervisor. And they buried the hunger artist along with the straw. But in his cage they put a young panther. Even for a person with the dullest mind it was clearly refreshing to see this wild animal throwing itself around in this cage, which had been dreary for such a long time. It lacked nothing. Without thinking about it for any length of time, the guards brought the animal food. It enjoyed the taste and never seemed to miss its freedom. This noble body, equipped with everything necessary, almost to the point of bursting, also appeared to carry freedom around with it. That seem to be located somewhere or other in its teeth, and its joy in living came with such strong passion from its throat that it was not easy for spectators to keep watching. But they controlled themselves, kept pressing around the cage, and had no desire to move on.

Story 6

A REPORT FOR AN ACADEMY

Esteemed Gentlemen of the Academy!

You show me the honour of calling upon me to submit a report to the Academy concerning my previous life as an ape.

In this sense, unfortunately, I cannot comply with your request. Almost five years separate me from my existence as an ape, a short time perhaps when measured by the calendar, but endlessly long to gallop through, as I have done, at times accompanied by splendid men, advice, applause, and orchestral music, but basically alone, since all those accompanying me held themselves back a long way from the barrier, in order to preserve the image. This achievement would have been impossible if I had stubbornly wished to hold onto my origin, onto the memories of my youth.

Giving up that obstinacy was, in fact, the highest command that I gave myself. I, a free ape, submitted myself to this yoke.

In so doing, however, my memories for their part constantly closed themselves off against me. If people had wanted it, my journey back at first would have been possible through the entire gateway which heaven builds over the earth, but as my development was whipped onwards, the gate simultaneously grew lower and narrower all the time. I felt myself more comfortable and more enclosed in the world of human beings. The storm which blew me out of my past eased off. Today it is only a gentle breeze which cools my heels. And the distant hole through which it comes and through which I once came has become so small that, even if I had sufficient power and will to run back there, I would have to scrape the fur off my body in order to get through. Speaking frankly, as much as I like choosing metaphors for these things—speaking frankly: your experience as apes, gentlemen—to the extent that you have something of that sort behind you—cannot be more distant from you than mine is from me. But it tickles at the heels of everyone who walks here on earth, the small chimpanzee as well as the great Achilles.

In the narrowest sense, however, I can perhaps answer your question, nonetheless, and indeed I do so with great pleasure.

The first thing I learned was to give a handshake. The handshake displays candour. Today, when I stand at the highpoint of my career, may I add to that first handshake also my candid words. For the Academy it will not provide anything essentially new and will fall far short of what people have asked of me and what with the best will I cannot speak about—but nonetheless it should demonstrate the line by which someone who was an ape was forced into the world of men and which he has continued there. Yet I would certainly not permit myself to say even the trivial things which follow if I were not completely sure of myself and if my position on all the great music hall stages of the civilized world had not established itself unassailably.

I come from the Gold Coast.

For an account of how I was captured I rely on the reports of strangers. A hunting expedition from the firm of Hagen back—incidentally, since then I have already emptied a number of bottles of good red wine with the leader of that expedition—lay hidden in the bushes by the shore when I ran down in the evening in the middle of a band of apes for a drink. Someone fired a shot. I was the only one struck. I received two hits.

One was in the cheek—that was superficial. But it left behind a large hairless red scar which earned me the name Red Peter—a revolting name, completely inappropriate, presumably something invented by an ape, as if the only difference between me and the recently deceased trained ape Peter, who was well known here and there, was the red patch on my cheek. But this is only by the way.

The second shot hit me below the hip. It was serious. It's the reason that today I still limp a little. Recently I read in an article by one of the ten thousand gossipers who vent their opinions about me in the newspapers that my ape nature is not yet entirely repressed. The proof is that when visitors come I take pleasure in pulling off my trousers to show the entry wound caused by this shot. That fellow should have each finger of his writing hand shot off one by one. So far as I am concerned, I may pull my trousers down in front of anyone I like. People will not find there anything other than well cared for fur and the scar from—let us select here a precise word for a precise purpose, something that will not be misunderstood—the scar from a wicked shot. Everything is perfectly open; there is nothing to hide. When it comes to a question of the truth, every great mind discards the most subtle refinements of manners. However, if that writer were to pull down his trousers when he gets a visitor, that would certainly produce a different sight, and I'll take it as a sign of reason that he does not do that. But then he should not bother me with his delicate sensibilities.

After those shots I woke up—and here my own memory gradually begins—in a cage between decks on the Hagen beck steamship. It was no four sided cage with bars, but only three walls fixed to a crate, so that the crate constituted the fourth wall. The whole thing was too low to stand upright and too narrow for sitting down. So I crouched with bent knees, which shook all the time, and since at first I probably did not wish to see anyone and to remain constantly in the darkness, I turned towards the crate, while the bars of the cage cut into the flesh on my back. People consider such confinement of wild animals beneficial in the very first period of time, and today I cannot deny, on the basis of my own experience, that in a human sense that is, in fact, the case.

But at that time I didn't think about it. For the first time in my life I was without a way out—at least there was no direct way out. Right in front of me was the crate, its boards fitted closely together.

Well, there was a hole running right through the boards. When I first discovered it, I welcomed it with a blissfully happy howl of ignorance. But this hole was not nearly big enough to stick my tail through, and all the power of an ape could not make it any bigger.

According to what I was told later, I am supposed to have made remarkably little noise. From that people concluded that either I must soon die or, if I succeeded in surviving the first critical period, I would be very capable of being trained. I survived this period. Muffled sobbing, painfully searching out fleas, wearily licking a coconut, banging my skull against the wall of the crate, sticking out my tongue when anyone came near—these were the first occupations in my new life. In all of them, however, there was only one feeling: no way out. Nowadays, of course, I can portray those ape like feelings only with human words and, as a result, I misrepresent them. But even if I can no longer attain the old truth of the ape, at least it lies in the direction I have described—of that there is no doubt.

Up until then I had had so many ways out, and now I no longer had one. I was tied down. If they had nailed me down, my freedom to move would not have been any less. And why? If you scratch raw the flesh between your toes, you won't find the reason. If you press your back against the bars of the cage until it almost slices you in two, you won't find the answer. I had no way out, but I had to come up with one for myself. For without that I could not live. Always in front of that crate wall—I would inevitably have died a miserable death. But according to Hagen beck, apes belong at the crate wall—well, that meant I had to cease being an ape. A clear and beautiful train of thought, which I must have planned somehow with my belly, since apes think with their bellies.

I'm worried that people do not understand precisely what I mean by a way out. I use the word in its most common and fullest sense. I am deliberately not saying freedom. I do not mean this great feeling of freedom on all sides. As an ape, I perhaps recognized it, and I have met human beings who yearn for it. But as far as I am concerned, I did not demand freedom either then or today. Incidentally, among human beings people all too often are deceived by freedom. And since freedom is reckoned among the most sublime feelings, the corresponding disappointment is also among the most sublime. In the variety shows, before my entrance, I have often watched a pair of artists busy on trapezes high up in the roof. They swung themselves, they rocked back and forth, they jumped, they hung in each other's arms, one held the other by clenching the hair with his teeth. "That, too, is human freedom," I thought, "self-controlled movement."

What a mockery of sacred nature! At such a sight, no structure would stand up to the laughter of the apes.

No, I didn't want freedom.

Only a way out—to the right or left or anywhere at all. I made no other demands, even if the way out should be only an illusion. The demand was small; the disappointment would not be any greater—to move on further, to move on further! Only not to stand still with arms raised, pressed again a crate wall.

Today I see clearly that without the greatest inner calm I would never have been able to get out. And in fact I probably owe everything that I have become to the calmness which came over me after the first days there on the ship. And, in turn, I owe that calmness to the people on the ship.

They are good people, in spite of everything. Today I still enjoy remembering the clang of their heavy steps, which used to echo then in my half sleep. They had the habit of tackling everything extremely slowly. If one of them wanted to rub his eyes, he raised his hand as if it were a hanging weight. Their jokes were gross but hearty. Their laughter was always mixed with a rasp which sounded dangerous but meant nothing. They always had something in their mouths to spit out, and they didn't care where they spat. They always complained that my fleas sprung over onto them, but they were never seriously angry at me because of it. They even knew that fleas liked being in my fur and that fleas are jumpers. They learned to live with that. When they had no duties, sometimes a few of them sat down in a semi circle around me. They didn't speak much, but only made noises to each other and smoked their pipes, stretched out on the crates. They slapped their knees as soon as I made the slightest movement, and from time to time one of them would pick up a stick and tickle me where I liked it. If I were invited today to make a journey on that ship, I'd certainly decline the invitation, but it's equally certain that the memories I could dwell on of the time there between the decks would not be totally hateful.

The calmness which I acquired in this circle of people prevented me above all from any attempt to escape. Looking at it nowadays, it seems to me as if I had at least sensed that I had to find a way out if I wanted to live, but that this way out could not be reached by escaping. I no longer know if escape was possible, but I think it was: for an ape it should always be possible to flee. With my present teeth I have to be careful even with the ordinary task of cracking a nut, but then I must have been able, over time, to succeed in chewing through the lock on the door. I didn't do that. What would I have achieved by doing that? No sooner would I have stuck my head out, than they would have captured me again and locked me up in an even worse cage. Or I could have taken refuge unnoticed among the other animals—say, the boa constrictors opposite me—and breathed my last in their embraces. Or I could have managed to steal way up to the deck and jumped overboard. Then I'd have tossed back and forth for a while on the ocean and drowned. Acts of despair.

I did not think things through in such a human way, but under the influence of my surroundings conducted myself as if I had worked things out.

I did not work things out, but I observed well in complete tranquility. I saw these men going back and forth, always the same faces, the same movements. Often it seemed to me as if there was only one man. So the man or these men went undisturbed. A lofty purpose dawned on me. No one promised me that if I could become like them the cage would be removed. Such promises, apparently impossible to fulfill, were not made. But if one makes the fulfillment good, then later the promises appear precisely there where one had looked for them earlier without success. Now, these men in themselves were nothing which attracted me very much. If I had been a follower of that freedom I just mentioned, I would certainly have preferred the ocean to the way out displayed in the dull gaze of these men. But in any case, I observed them for a long time before I even thought about such things—in fact, the accumulated observations first pushed me in the proper direction.

It was so easy to imitate these people. I could already spit on the first day. We used to spit in each other's faces. The only difference was that I licked my face clean afterwards. They did not. Soon I was smoking a pipe, like an old man, and if I then pressed my thumb down into the bowl of the pipe, the entire area between decks cheered. Still, for a long time I did not understand the difference between an empty and a full pipe.

I had the greatest difficulty with the bottle of alcohol. The smell was torture to me. I forced myself with all my power, but weeks went by before I could overcome my reaction. Curiously enough, the people took this inner struggle more seriously than anything else about me. In my memories I don't distinguish the people, but there was one who always came back, alone or with comrades, day and night, at different times. He'd stand with a bottle in front of me and give me instructions. He did not understand me. He wanted to solve the riddle of my being. He used to uncork the bottle slowly and then look at me, in order to test if I had understood. I confess that I always looked at him with wildly over eager attentiveness. No human teacher has ever found in the entire world such a student of human beings.

After he'd uncorked the bottle, he'd raise it to his mouth. I'd gaze at him, right at his throat. He would nod, pleased with me, and set the bottle to his lips. Delighted with my gradual understanding, I'd squeal and scratch myself all over, wherever it was convenient. He was happy. He'd set the bottle to his mouth and take a swallow. Impatient and desperate to emulate him,

I would defecate over myself in my cage—and that again gave him great satisfaction.

Then, holding the bottle at arm's length and bringing it up again with a swing, he'd drink it down with one gulp, exaggerating his backward bending as a way of instructing me. Exhausted with so much great effort, I could no longer follow and hung weakly onto the bars, while he ended the theoretical lesson by rubbing his belly and grinning.

Now the practical exercises first began. Was I not already too tired out by the theoretical part? Yes, indeed, far too weary. That's part of my fate. Nonetheless, I'd grab the proffered bottle as well as I could and uncork it trembling. Once I'd managed to do that, new forces gradually take over. I lift the bottle—with hardly any difference between me and the original—put it to my lips—and throw it away in disgust, in disgust, although it is empty and filled only with the smell, throw it with disgust onto the floor. To the sorrow of my teacher, to my own greater sorrow. And I still do not console him or myself when, after throwing away the bottle, I do not forget to give my belly a splendid rub and to grin as I do so.

All too often, the lesson went that way. And to my teacher's credit, he was not angry with me. Well, sometimes he held his burning pipe against my fur in some place or other which I could reach only with difficulty, until it began to burn. But then he would put it out himself with his huge good hand. He wasn't angry with me. He realized that we were fighting on the same side against ape nature and that I had the more difficult part.

What a victory it was for him and for me, however, when one evening in front of a large circle of onlookers—perhaps it was a celebration, a gramophone was playing, and officer was wandering around among the people—when on this evening, at a moment when no one was watching, I grabbed a bottle of alcohol which had been inadvertently left standing in front of my cage, uncorked it just as I had been taught, amid the rising attention of the group, set it against my mouth and, without hesitating, with my mouth making no grimace, like an expert drinker, with my eyes rolling around, splashing the liquid in my throat, I really and truly drank the bottle empty, and then threw it away, no longer in despair, but like an artist. Well, I did forget to scratch my belly. But instead of that, because I couldn't do anything else, because I had to, because my senses were roaring, I cried out a short and good "Hello!" breaking out into human sounds. And with this cry I sprang into the community of human beings, and I felt its echo—"Just listen. He's talking!"—like a kiss on my entire sweat soaked body.

I'll say it again: imitating human beings was not something which pleased me. I imitated them because I was looking for a way out, for no other reason. And even in that victory little was achieved. My voice immediately failed me again. It first came back months later. My distaste for the bottle of alcohol became even stronger. But at least my direction was given to me once and for all.

When I was handed over in Hamburg to my first trainer, I soon realized the two possibilities open to me: the Zoological Garden or the Music Hall. I did not hesitate. I said to myself: use all your energy to get into the Music Hall. That is the way out. The Zoological Garden is only a new barred cage. If you go there, you're lost.

And I learned, gentlemen. Alas, one learns when one has to. One learns when one wants a way out. One learns ruthlessly. One supervises oneself with a whip and tears oneself apart at the slightest resistance. My ape nature ran off, head over heels, out of me, so that in the process my first teacher himself almost became an ape and soon had to give up training and be carried off to a mental hospital. Fortunately he was soon discharged again.

But I went through many teachers—indeed, even several teachers at once. As I became more confident of my abilities and the general public followed my progress and my future began to brighten, I took on teachers myself, let them sit down in five interconnected rooms, and studied with them all simultaneously, by constantly leaping from one room into another.

And such progress! The penetrating effects of the rays of knowledge from all sides on my awaking brain! I don't deny the fact—I was delighted with it. But I also confess that I did not overestimate it, not even then, even less today. With an effort which up to this point has never been repeated on earth, I have attained the average education of a European. That would perhaps not amount to much, but it is something insofar as it helped me out of the cage and created this special way out for me—the way out of human beings. There is an excellent German expression: to beat one's way through the bushes. That I have done. I have beaten my way through the bushes. I had no other way, always assuming that freedom was not a choice.

If I review my development and its goal up to this point, I do not complain. I am even satisfied. With my hands in my trouser pockets, the bottle of wine on the table, I half lie and half sit in my rocking chair and gaze out the window. If I have a visitor, I welcome him as is appropriate. My impresario sits in the parlour. If I ring, he comes and listens to what I have to say. In the evening I almost always have a performance, and my success could hardly rise any higher. When I come home late from banquets, from scientific societies, or from social gatherings in someone's home, a small half-trained female chimpanzee is waiting for me, and I take my pleasure with her the way apes do. During the day I don't want to see her. For she has in her gaze the madness of a bewildered trained animal. I'm the only one who recognizes that, and I cannot bear it.

On the whole, at any rate, I have achieved what I wished to achieve. You shouldn't say it wasn't worth the effort. In any case, I don't want any man's judgment. I only want to expand knowledge. I simply report.

Even to you, esteemed gentlemen of the Academy, I have only made a report.

Story 7

THE JUDGEMENT

It was a Sunday morning at the most beautiful time in spring. George Benderman, a young merchant, was sitting in his private room on the first floor of one of the low, poorly constructed houses extending in a long row along the river, almost indistinguishable from each other except for their height and colour. He had just finished a letter to a friend from his youth who was now abroad, had sealed in a playful and desultory manner, and then was looking, elbows propped on the writing table, out of the window at the river, the bridge, and the hills on the other shore with their delicate greenery.

He was thinking about how this friend, dissatisfied with his progress at home, had actually run off to Russia some years before. Now he ran a business in St. Petersburg, which had gotten off to a very good start but which for a long time now had appeared to be faltering, as his friend complained on his increasingly rare visits. So he was wearing himself out working to no purpose in a foreign land. The exotic full beard only poorly concealed the face George had known so well since his childhood years, and the yellowish colour of his skin seemed to indicate a developing sickness. As he explained it, he had no real connection to the colony of his countrymen in the place and also hardly any social interaction with local families and so was resigning himself to being a permanent bachelor.

What should one write to such a man, who had obviously gone off course, a man one could feel sorry for but could not help. Should one perhaps advise him to come back home again, shift his life back here, take up again all the old friendly relationships—there was certainly nothing to prevent that—and in addition rely on the help of friends? But that amounted to the same thing as saying to him—and the more gently one said it, the more wounding it would also be—that his previous attempts had been unsuccessful, that he should finally give them up, that he must come back and allow everyone to gape at him as an eternal returned prodigal, that only his friends understood anything, and that he would be an overage child, who should simply obey his successful friends who had stayed home. And then was it certain that all the misery one would have to put him through had a point? Perhaps it would not even succeed in bringing him back home at all—he said himself that he no longer understood conditions in his homeland—so then he would remain in his foreign country in spite of everything, embittered by the advice and a little more estranged from his friends.

But if he really followed the advice and became depressed here—not intentionally, of course, but because of his circumstances—could not cope with life, with his friends or without them, felt ashamed, and had, in fact, no homeland and no friends any more, was it not much better for him to remain abroad, just as he was? Given these facts, could one think that he would really advance himself here?

For these reasons, if one still wanted to maintain some sort of relationship by correspondence, one could not provide any real news, the way one would without any inhibitions to the most casual acquaintance. It was already more than three years since his friend had been home, and he explained this with the very inadequate excuse of the uncertainty of the political conditions in Russia, which would not allow even the briefest absence of a small businessman, while it permitted hundreds of thousands of Russians to travel around peacefully in the world. But in the course of these three years much had changed for George. Since his mother's death, which had taken place about two years earlier, George had lived with his old father in a household they shared. His friend had naturally learned about it and had expressed his sympathy in a letter with such a dry tone that the reason could only have been that the sadness of such an event is completely inconceivable in a foreign country. But since that time George had tackled both his business dealings and everything else with greater determination. Perhaps while his mother was still alive, his father's unwillingness to accept any point of view in the business except his had prevented George from developing a real project of his own; perhaps his father, since his mother's death, had grown slacker, although he still worked all the time in the business; perhaps fortunate circumstances had played a much more important role—something which was, in fact, highly likely—but in any case in these two years the business had developed very unexpectedly. They had had to double the staff, the cash turnover had increased fivefold, and there was no doubt that further progress lay ahead.

His friend, however, had no idea of these changes. Earlier, perhaps for the last time in that letter of condolence, he had wanted to persuade George to emigrate to Russia and had expanded upon the prospects which existed in St. Petersburg for George's particular line of business. The figures were minute compared to the scale which George's business had now acquired. But George had had no desire to write to his friend about his commercial success, and if he were to do it now belatedly, it would have looked really odd.

So George limited himself to writing to his friend only about insignificant details, the kind which pile up at random in one's memory when one is thinking things over on a peaceful Sunday. The only thing he wanted was to leave undisturbed the picture which his friend must have created of his home town during the long interval and which he would have learned to live with.

And so it happened that George had announced three times to his friend in fairly widely spaced letters the engagement of an unimportant man to an equally unimportant young woman, until, quite contrary to George's intentions, the friend really began to get interested in this curious event.

But George preferred to write to him about such things rather than to confess that he himself had become engaged a month ago to a Miss Frieda Brandenfeld, a young woman from a prosperous family. He often spoke to his fiancée about this friend and about the unusual relationship he had with him in their correspondence. "Then there's no chance he'll be coming to our wedding," she said, "and yet I have the right to meet all your friends." "I don't want to upset him," George replied. "Don't misunderstand me. He would probably come, at least I think so, but he would feel compelled and hurt and would perhaps envy me—he'd certainly feel unhappy and incapable of ever coping with his unhappiness and would travel back alone. Alone—do you know what that means?" "Yes, but can't he find out about our wedding in some other way?" "That's true, but I can't prevent that. However, given his lifestyle it's unlikely." "If you have friends like that, George, you shouldn't have gotten engaged at all." "Well, we're both to blame for that, but now I wouldn't want things to be any different." And then when she, breathing rapidly under his kisses, kept insisting "Still, it truly does upset me," he really thought it would be harmless to write everything to his friend. "That's what I am and that's just how he'll have to accept me," he said to himself. "I can't carve out of myself another man who might perhaps be more suitable for a friendship with him than I am."

And, in fact, he did inform his friend about the engagement which had taken place in the long letter which he had written that Sunday morning, in the following words "The best piece of news I have saved until the end. I have become engaged to a Miss Frieda Brandenfeld, a young woman from a well-to-do family, who first settled here long after your departure and thus whom you could hardly know. There will still be an opportunity to tell you more detailed information about my fiancée. Today it's enough for you to know that I am truly fortunate and that, as far as our mutual relationship is concerned, the only thing that has changed is that in me you will now have, instead of a completely ordinary friend, a happy friend. Moreover, in my fiancée, who sends her warm greetings and will soon write to you herself, you acquire a sincere female friend, something which is not entirely without significance for a bachelor. I know that there are many things hindering you from coming back to visit us, but wouldn't my wedding be exactly the right opportunity to throw aside these obstacles for once? But whatever the case, do what seems good to you, without concerning yourself about anything"

George sat for a long time at his writing table with his letter in his hand, his face turned towards the window. He barely acknowledged with an absent minded smile someone he knew who greeted him from the lane as he walked past.

Finally he put the letter in his pocket and went out of his room, angling across a small passageway into his father's room, which he had not been in for months. There was really no need to do that, since he was always dealing with his father at work and they took their noon meal at the same time in a restaurant.

In the evenings, of course, they each did as they wished, but for the most part, unless George was with friends, as was most frequently the case, or was now visiting his fiancée, they still sat for a little while, each with his own newspaper, in the living room they shared.

George was surprised how dark his father's room was, even on this sunny morning. So that was the kind of shadow cast by the high wall which rose on the other side of the narrow courtyard. His father was sitting by the window in a corner decorated with various reminders of his late lamented mother and was reading a newspaper, which he held in front of his eyes to one side, attempting in this way to compensate for some weakness in his eyes. On the table stood the remains of his breakfast, not much of which appeared to have been eaten.

"Ah, George," said his father, coming up at once to meet him. His heavy night shirt opened up as he moved and the ends of it flapped around him. "My father is still a giant," said George to himself.

Then he spoke up: "It's unbearably dark in here."

"Yes, it certainly is dark," his father answered.

"And you've shut the window as well?"

"I prefer it that way."

"Well, it is quite warm outside," said George, as if continuing what he'd said earlier, and sat down.

His father cleared off the breakfast dishes and put them on a cupboard.

"I really only wanted to tell you," continued George, who was following the movements of the old man quite absent minded, "that I've now sent a report of my engagement to St. Petersburg." He pulled the letter a little way out of his pocket and let it drop back again.

"Why to St. Petersburg?" his father asked.

"To my friend," said George, trying to look his father in the eye. "In business he's completely different," he thought. "How sturdily he sits here with his arms across his chest."

"Ah yes, to your friend," said his father, with emphasis.

"Well, father, you know at first I wanted to keep quiet to him about my engagement. Out of consideration, for no other reason. You yourself know he's a difficult person. I said to myself he could well learn about my engagement from some other quarter, even if his solitary way of life makes that hardly likely—I can't prevent that—but he should never learn about it from me."

"And now you're thinking about it differently?" the father asked. He set the large newspaper on the window sill and on top the newspaper his glasses, which he covered with his hand.

"Yes, now I've been reconsidering it.

If he's a good friend of mine, I said to myself, then a happy engagement for me is also something fortunate for him. And so I no longer hesitated to announce it to him. But before I send the letter, I wanted to tell you about it."

"George," said his father, pulling his toothless mouth wide open, "listen to me! You've come to me about this matter, to discuss it with me. No doubt that's a credit to you. But it's nothing, worse than nothing if you don't now tell me the complete truth. I don't want to stir up things which are not appropriate here. Since the death of our dear mother certain nasty things have been going on. Perhaps the time to talk about them has come and perhaps sooner than we think. In the business, a good deal escapes me. Perhaps it's not hidden from me—at the moment I'm not claiming it's done behind my back—I am no longer strong enough, my memory is deteriorating, I can't keep an eye on so many things any more. First of all, that's nature taking its course, and secondly the death of our dear mother was a much bigger blow to me than to you. But since we're on the subject of this letter, I beg you, George, don't deceive me. It's a trivial thing, not worth mentioning. So don't deceive me. Do you really have this friend in St. Petersburg?"

George stood up in embarrassment. "Let's forget about my friend. A thousand friends wouldn't replace my father for me. Do you know what I think? You're not taking enough care of yourself. But old age demands its due. You are indispensable to me in the business—you're very well aware of that—but if the business is going to threaten your health, I'll close it tomorrow for good. That won't happen. We must set up a different life style for you. But something completely different. You sit here in the dark, and in the living room you'd have good light. You nibble at your breakfast instead of maintaining your strength properly. You sit by the closed window, and the air would do you so much good. No, my father! I'll bring in the doctor, and we'll follow his instructions. We'll change your room. You'll move into the front room. I'll come in here. For you there won't be any change. Everything will be moved over with you. But there's time for all hat. Now I'll see you in bed for a little while. You need complete rest. Come, I'll help you get undressed. You'll see. I can do it. Or do you want to go into the front room right away. Then you can lie down in my bed for now. That would make a lot of sense."

George stood close beside his father, who had let his head with its tousled white hair sink onto his chest.

"George," said his father faintly, without moving.

George knelt down immediately alongside his father. He saw the enormous pupils in his father's tired face staring right at him from the corners of his eyes.

"You don't have a friend in St. Petersburg. You have always been a jokester and even with me you've not controlled yourself. So how could you have a friend there! I simply can't believe that.

"Think about it for a moment, father," said George. He raised his father from the arm chair and took off his nightgown as he just stood there very weakly. "It will soon be almost three years since my friend visited us. I still remember that you did not particularly like him. At least twice I kept him away from you, although he was sitting right in my room. It's true I could understand your aversion to him quite well. My friend does have his peculiarities. But then you later had a really good conversation with him yourself. At the time I was so proud of the fact that you listened to him, nodded your head, and asked questions. If you think about it, you must remember. That's when he told us some incredible stories about the Russian Revolution. For example, on a business trip in Kiev during a riot he saw a priest on a balcony who cut a wide bloody cross into the palm of his hand, raised his hand and appealed to the mob. You've even repeated this story yourself now and then."

Meanwhile, George had succeeded in setting his father down again and carefully taking off the cotton trousers which he wore over his linen underwear, as well as his socks. Looking at the undergarments, which were not particularly clean, he reproached himself for having neglected his father. It certainly should have been his responsibility to look after his father's changes in underwear. He had not yet talked explicitly with his fiancée about how they wished to make arrangements for his father's future, for they had tacitly assumed that his father would remain living alone in the old apartment. But now he quickly came to the firm decision to take his father with him into his future household. When one looked more closely, it almost seemed that the care which he was ready to provide for his father there could come too late. He carried his father to bed in his arms. He experienced a dreadful feeling when he noticed, as he took a couple of paces to the bed, that his father was playing with the watch chain on his chest.

He could not put him in the bed right away, so firm was his father's grip on this watch chain.

But as soon as he was in bed, all seemed well. He covered himself up and then even pulled the bedspread unusually high up over his shoulders. He look up at George in a not unfriendly manner.

"You do still remember him, don't you?" said George, nodding his head in encouragement.

"Am I well covered up now?" asked the father, as if he could not check whether his feet were sufficiently tucked in.

"So you feel good in bed now," said George and arranged the bedding better around him.

"Am I well covered up?" the father asked once more and seemed particularly keen to hear the answer.

"Just rest for now. You're well covered up."

"No!" cried his father, cutting short George's answer to the question.

He threw back the covers with such force that in an instant they had completely flown off, and stood upright on the bed. He steadied himself with only one hand lightly touching the ceiling. "You wanted to cover me up—I know that, my little offspring—but I am not yet under the covers. And even if this is the last strength I have, it's enough for you, too much for you. Yes, I do know your friend. He'd be a son after my own heart. That's why you've been betraying him for years. Why else? Do you think I've not wept for him? That's the reason you lock yourself in your office—no one should disturb you, the boss is busy—that's the only way you can write your two faced little letters to Russia. But fortunately no one has to teach a father to see through his son. Just now when you thought you'd brought him down, so far down that your buttocks could sit on him and he wouldn't move, at that point my son the gentleman has decided to get married!"

George looked up at the frightening spectre of his father. The friend in St. Petersburg, whom the father suddenly knew so well, seized his imagination as never before. He saw him lost in the broad expanse of Russia. He saw him at the door of an empty, plundered business. Among the wreckage of his shelves, the shattered goods, the collapsed gas brackets, he was still standing, but only just. Why did he have to go so far away!

"But look at me," cried his father, and George ran, almost distracted, to the bed to take everything in, but he faltered half way. "Because she hoisted up her skirts," the father began in an affected tone, "because she hoisted up her skirts like this, the repulsive goose," and in order to imitate the action, he raised his shirt so high one could see the scar from his war years on his thigh, "because she hoisted her dress up like this and this, you chatted her up, and that's how you could satisfy yourself with her without being disturbed—you've disgraced our mother's memory, betrayed your friend, and stuck your father in bed, so he can't move. But he can move, can't he?" And he stood completely unsupported and kicked his legs. He was radiant with insight.

George stood in a corner, as far away as possible from his father. A long time before he had firmly decided to observe everything closely, so he would not be surprised somehow by any devious attack, from behind or from above. Now he recalled again this long forgotten decision and forgot it, like someone pulling a short thread through the eye of a needle.

"But now your friend hasn't been betrayed at all," cried the father—his forefinger, waving back and forth, emphasized the point. "I've been his on-the-spot representative here".

"You comedian!" George could not resist calling out. He recognized immediately how damaging that was and bit down on his tongue, only too late—his eyes froze—until he doubled up with pain.

"Yes, naturally I've been playing a comedy! Comedy! A fine word! What other consolation remained for an old widowed father? Tell me—and while you're answering be my still living son—what else was left to me in my back room, persecuted by a disloyal staff, old right down into to my bones? And my son goes merrily through the world, finishing off business deals which I had set up, falling over himself with delight, and walking away from your father with the tight-lipped face of an honourable gentleman! Do you think I didn't love you, me, the one from whom you came?"

"Now he'll bend forward," thought George. "What if he falls and breaks apart!" These words hissed through his head.

His father leaned forward but did not fall over. When George did not come closer, as he had expected, he straightened himself up again.

"Stay where you are. I don't need you! You think you still have the strength to come here and are holding yourself back only because that's what you want. But what if you're wrong! I am still much stronger than you. Perhaps all on my own I would have to have had to back off, but your mother gave me so much of her strength that I've established a splendid relationship with your friend and I have your customers here in my pocket!"

"He even has pockets in his shirt!" said George to himself and thought with this comment he could make his father look ridiculous to the whole world. He thought this for only a moment, because he constantly forgot everything.

"Just link arms with your fiancée and cross my path! I'll sweep her right from your side—you have no idea how!"

George made a grimace, as if he didn't believe that. The father merely nodded towards George's corner, emphasizing the truth of what he'd said.

"How you amused me today when you came and asked whether you should write to your friend about the engagement. For he knows everything, you stupid boy, he already knows everything! I've been writing to him, because you forgot to take my writing things away from me. That's why he hasn't come for years. He knows everything a hundred times better than you do yourself. He crumples up your letters unread in his left hand, while in his right hand he holds my letters up to read."

In his enthusiasm he swung his arm over his head. "He knows everything a thousand times better," he shouted.

"Ten thousand times," said George, in order to make his father appear foolish, but in his mouth the phrase had already acquired a deathly tone.

"For years now I've been watching out for you to come with this question! Do you think I'm concerned about anything else? Do you think I read the newspapers? There!" and he threw a newspaper page which had somehow been carried into the bed right at George—an old newspaper, the name of which was completely unknown to George.

"How long you've waited before reaching maturity! Your mother had to die. She could not experience the joyous day.

Your friend is deteriorating in his Russia—three years ago he was already yellow enough to be thrown away, and, as for me, well, you see how things are with me. You've got eyes for that!"

"So you've been lying in wait for me," cried George.

In a pitying tone, his father said as an afterthought, "Presumably you wanted to say that earlier. But now it's totally irrelevant."

And in a louder voice: "So now you know what there was in the world outside of yourself. Up to this point you've known only about yourself! Essentially you've been an innocent child, but even more essentially you've been a devilish human being! And therefore understand this: I sentence you now to death by drowning!"

George felt himself hounded from the room. The crash with which his father fell onto the bed behind him he still carried in his ears as he left. On the staircase, where he raced down the steps as if it were an inclined plane, he surprised his cleaning woman, who was intending to tidy the apartment after the night before.

"Jesus!" she cried and hid her face in her apron. But he was already past her. He leapt out the front door, driven across the roadway to the water. He was already clutching the railings the way a starving man grasps his food. He swung himself over, like the outstanding gymnast he had been in his youth, to his parents' pride. He was still holding on, his grip weakening, when between the railings he caught sight of a motor coach which would easily drown out the noise of his fall. He called out quietly, "Dear parents, I have always loved you nonetheless" and let himself drop.

At that moment an almost unending stream of traffic was going over the bridge.

Story 8

THE HUNTER GRACCHUS

Two boys were sitting on the wall by the jetty playing dice. A man was reading a newspaper on the steps of a monument in the shadow of a hero wielding a sabre. A young girl was filling her tub with water at a fountain. A fruit seller was lying close to his produce and looking out to sea. Through the empty openings of the door and window of a bar two men could be seen drinking wine in the back. The landlord was sitting at a table in the front dozing. A small boat glided lightly into the small harbour, as if it were being carried over the water. A man in a blue jacket climbed out onto land and pulled the ropes through the rings. Behind the man from the boat, two other men in dark coats with silver buttons carried a bier, on which, under a large silk scarf with a floral pattern and fringe, a man was obviously lying.

No one bothered with the newcomers on the jetty, even when they set the bier down to wait for their helmsman, who was still working with the ropes. No one came up to them, no one asked them any questions, no one took a closer look at them.

The helmsman was further held up a little by a woman with disheveled hair, who now appeared on deck with a child at her breast. Then he came on, pointing to a yellowish two story house which rose close by, directly on the left near the water. The bearers took up their load and carried it through the low door furnished with slender columns. A small boy opened a window, noticed immediately how the group was disappearing into the house, and quickly shut the window again. The door closed. It had been fashioned with care out of black oak wood. A flock of doves, which up to this point had been flying around the bell tower, came down in front of the house. The doves gathered before the door, as if their food was stored inside the house. One flew right up to the first floor and pecked at the window pane. They were brightly coloured, well cared for, lively animals. With a large sweep of her hand the woman on the boat threw some seeds towards them. They ate them up and then flew over to the woman.

A man in a top hat with a mourning ribbon came down one of the small, narrow, steeply descending lanes which led to the harbour. He looked around him attentively. Everything upset him. He winced at the sight of some garbage in a corner. There were fruit peels on the steps of the monument. As he went by, he pushed them off with his cane. He knocked on the door of the house, while at the same time taking off his top hat with his black gloved right hand. It was opened immediately, and about fifty small boys, lined up in two rows in a long corridor, bowed to him.

The helmsman came down the stairs, met the gentleman, and led him upstairs.

On the first floor he accompanied him around the slight, delicately built balcony surrounding the courtyard, and, as the boys crowded behind them at a respectful distance, both men stepped into a large cool room at the back. From it one could not see a facing house, only a bare gray black rock wall. Those who had carried the bier were busy setting up and lighting some long candles at its head. But these provided no light. They only made the previously still shadows jump and flicker across the walls. The shawl was pulled back off the bier. On it lay a man with wildly unkempt hair and beard and a brown skin—he looked rather like a hunter. He lay there motionless, apparently without breathing, his eyes closed, although his surroundings were the only the only thing indicating that it could be a corpse.

The gentleman stepped over to the bier, laid a hand on the forehead of the man lying there, then knelt down and prayed. The helmsman gave a sign to the bearers to leave the room. They went out, drove away the boys who had gathered outside, and shut the door. The gentleman, however, was apparently still not satisfied with this stillness. He looked at the helmsman. The latter understood and went through a side door into the next room. The man on the bier immediately opened his eyes, turned his face with a painful smile towards the gentleman, and said, "Who are you?" Without any surprise, the gentleman got up from his kneeling position and answered, "The burgomaster of Riva."

The man on the bier nodded, pointed to a chair by stretching his arm out feebly, and then, after the burgomaster had accepted his invitation, said, "Yes, I knew that, Burgomaster, but when I first glance around I've always forgotten it all—everything is going in circles around me, and it's better for me to ask, even when I know everything. You also presumably know that I am the hunter Gracchus."

"Of course," said the burgomaster. "I received the news today, during the night. We had been sleeping for some time. Then around midnight my wife called, 'Salvatore'—that's my name—'look at the dove in the window!' It was really a dove, but as large as a rooster. It flew up to my ear and said, 'Tomorrow the dead hunter Gracchus is coming. Welcome him in the name of the city'."

The hunter nodded and pushed the tip of his tongue between his lips. "Yes, the doves fly here before me. But do you believe, Burgomaster, that I am to remain in Riva?"

"That I cannot yet say," answered the burgomaster. "Are you dead?"

"Yes," said the hunter, "as you see. Many years ago—it must have been a great many years ago—I fell from a rock in the Black Forest—that's in Germany—as I was tracking a chamois. Since then I've been dead."

"But you're also alive," said the burgomaster.

"To a certain extent," said the hunter, "to a certain extent I am also alive. My death ship lost its way—a wrong turn of the helm, a moment when the helmsman was not paying attention, a distraction from my wonderful homeland—I don't know what it was.

I only know that I remain on the earth and that since that time my ship has journeyed over earthly waters. So I—who only wanted to live in my own mountains—travel on after my death through all the countries of the earth."

"And have you no share in the world beyond?" asked the burgomaster wrinkling his brow.

The hunter answered, "I am always on the immense staircase leading up to it. I roam around on this infinitely wide flight of steps, sometimes up, sometimes down, sometimes to the right, sometimes to the left, always in motion. From being a hunter I've become a butterfly. Don't laugh."

"I'm not laughing," answered the burgomaster.

"That's very considerate of you," said the hunter. "I am always moving. But when I go through the greatest upward motion and the door is shining right above me, I wake up on my old ship, still drearily stranded in some earthly stretch of water. The basic mistake of my earlier death grins at me in my cabin. Julia, the wife of the helmsman, knocks and brings to me on the bier the morning drink of the country whose coast we are sailing by at the time. I lie on a wooden plank bed, wearing—I'm no delight to look at—a filthy shroud, my hair and beard, black and gray, are inextricably intertangled, my legs covered by a large silk women's scarf, with a floral pattern and long fringes. At my head stands a church candle which illuminates me. On the wall opposite me is a small picture, evidently of a bushman aiming his spear at me and concealing himself as much as possible behind a splendidly painted shield. On board ship one comes across many stupid pictures, but this is one of the stupidest. Beyond that my wooden cage is completely empty. Through a hole in the side wall the warm air of the southern nights comes in, and I hear the water lapping against the old boat.

I have been lying here since the time when I—the still living hunter Gracchus—was pursuing a chamois to its home in the Black Forest and fell. Everything took place as it should. I followed, fell down, bled to death in a ravine, was dead, and this boat was supposed to carry me to the other side. I still remember how happily I stretched myself out here on the planking for the first time. The mountains have never hear me singing the way these four still shadowy walls did then.

I had been happy to be alive and was happy to be dead. Before I came on board, I gladly threw away my rag-tag collection of guns and bags, even the hunting rifle which I had always carried so proudly, and slipped into the shroud like a young girl into her wedding dress. There I lay down and waited. Then the accident happened."

"A nasty fate," said the burgomaster, raising his hand in a gesture of depreciation, "and you are not to blame for it in any way?"

"No," said the hunter. "I was a hunter. Is there any blame in that? I was raised to be a hunter in the Black Forest, where at that time there were still wolves.

I lay in wait, shot, hit the target, removed the skin—is there any blame in that? My work was blessed. 'The great hunter of the Black Forest'—that's what they called me. Is that something bad?"

"It not up to me to decide that," said the burgomaster, "but it seems to me as well that there's no blame there. But then who is to blame?"

"The boatman," said the hunter. "No one will read what I write here, no one will come to help me. If people were assigned the task of helping me, all the doors of all the houses would remain closed, all the windows would be shut, they would all lie in bed, with sheets thrown over their heads, the entire earth would be a hostel for the night. And that makes good sense, for no one knows of me, and if he did, he would have no idea of where I was staying, and if he knew that, he would still not know how to keep me there, and so he would not know how to help me. The thought of wanting to help me is a sickness and has to be cured with bed rest.

"I know that, and so I do not cry out to summon help, even if at moments when I have no self-control, for example right now, I do think about that very seriously. But to get rid of such ideas I need only look around and recall where I am and where—and this I can assert with full confidence—I have lived for centuries.

"That's extraordinary," said the burgomaster, "extraordinary. And now are you intending to remain with us in Riva?"

"I have no intentions," said the hunter with a smile and, to make up for his mocking tone, laid a hand on the burgomaster's knee. "I am here. I don't know any more than that. There's nothing more I can do. My boat is without a helm—it journeys with the wind which blows in the deepest regions of death.

Story 9

REJECTION

When I meet a pretty girl and beg her: 'Be so good as to come with me,' and she walks past without a word, this is what she means to say:

'You are no Duke with a famous name, no broad American with a Red Indian figure, level, brooding eyes and a skin tempered by the air of the prairies and the rivers that flow through them, you have never journeyed to the seven seas and voyaged on them wherever they may be, I don't know where. So why, pray, should a pretty girl like myself go with you?'

'You forget that no automobile swings you through the street in long thrusts; I see no gentlemen escorting you in a close half circle, pressing on your skirts from behind and murmuring blessings on your head; your breasts are well placed into your bodice, but your thighs and hips make up for that restraint; you are wearing a taffeta dress with a pleated skirt such as delighted all of us last autumn, and yet you smile inviting mortal danger from time to time.'

'Yes, we're both in the right, and to keep us from being irrevocably aware of it, hadn't we better just go our separate ways home?'

Story 10

CHILDREN ON A COUNTRY ROAD

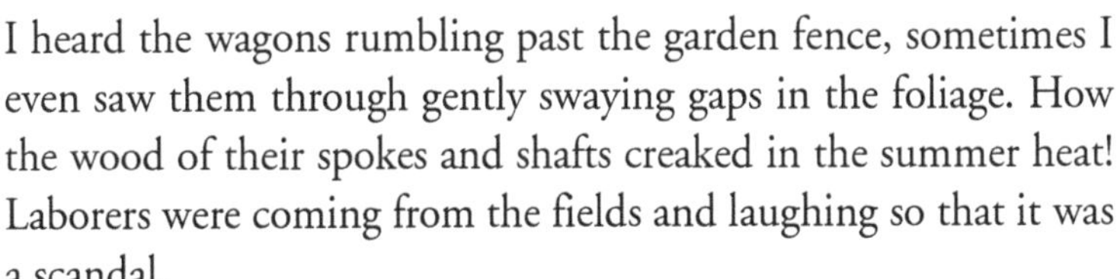

I heard the wagons rumbling past the garden fence, sometimes I even saw them through gently swaying gaps in the foliage. How the wood of their spokes and shafts creaked in the summer heat! Laborers were coming from the fields and laughing so that it was a scandal.

I was sitting on our little swing, just resting among the trees in my parents' garden.

On the other side of the fence the traffic never stopped. Children's running feet were past in a moment; harvest wagons with men and women perched on and around the sheaves darkened the flower beds; toward evening I saw a gentleman slowly promenading with a walking stick, and a couple of girls who met him arm in arm stepped aside into the grass as they greeted him.

Then birds flew up as if in showers, I followed them with my eyes and saw how high they soared in one breath, till I felt not that they were rising but that I was falling, and holding fast to the ropes began to swing a little out of sheer weakness. Soon I was swinging more strongly as the air blew colder and instead of soaring birds trembling stars appeared.

I was given my supper by candlelight. Often both my arms were on the wooden board and I was already weary as I bit into my bread and butter. The coarse mesh window curtains bellied in the warm wind and many a time some passer by outside would stay them with his hands as if he wanted to see me better and speak to me. Usually the candle soon went out and in the sooty candle smoke the assembled midges went on circling for a while. If anyone asked me a question from the window I would gaze at him as if at a distant mountain or into vacancy, nor did he particularly care whether he got an answer or not. But if one jumped over the window sill and announced that the others were already waiting, then I did get to my feet with a sigh.

'What are you sighing for? What's wrong? Has something dreadful happened that can never be made good? Shan't we ever recover from it? Is everything lost?'

Nothing was lost. We ran to the front of the house. 'Thank God, here you are at last!' – 'You're always late!' – 'Why just me?' – 'Especially you, why don't you stay at home if you don't want to come.' – 'No quarter!' – 'No quarter? What kind of way is that to talk?'

We ran our heads full tilt into the evening. There was no daytime and no night time. Now our waistcoat buttons would be clacking together like teeth, again we would be keeping a steady distance from each other as we ran, breathing fire like wild beasts in the tropics. Like cuirassiers in old wars, stamping and springing high, we drove each other down the short alley and with this impetus in our legs a farther stretch along the main road. Stray figures went into the ditch, hardly had they vanished down the dusky escarpment when they were standing like newcomers on the field path above and looking down.

'Come on down!' – 'Come on up first!' – 'So's you can push us down, no thanks, we're not such fools.' – 'You're afraid, you mean. Come on up, you cowards!' – 'Afraid? of the likes of you? You're going to push us down, are you? That's a good one.'

We made the attempt and were pushed head over heels into the grass of the roadside ditch, tumbling of our own free will. Everything was equally warm to us, we felt neither-warmth nor chill in the grass, only one got tired.

Turning on one's right side, with a hand under the ear, one could easily have fallen asleep there. But one wanted to get up again with chin uplifted, only to roll into a deeper ditch. Then with an arm thrust out crosswise and legs threshing to the side one thought to launch into the air again only to fall for certain into a still deeper ditch. And of this one never wanted to make an end.

How one might stretch oneself out, especially in the knees, properly to sleep in the last ditch, was something scarcely thought of, and one simply lay on one's back, like an invalid, inclined to weep a little. One blinked as now and then a youngster with elbows pressed to his sides sprang over one's head with dark looming soles, in a leap from the escarpment to the roadway.

The moon was already some way up in the sky, in its light a mail coach drove past. A small wind began to blow everywhere, even in the ditch one could feel it, and nearby the forest began to rustle. Then one was no longer so anxious to be alone.

'Where are you?' – 'Come here!' – 'All together!' – 'What are you hiding for, drop your nonsense!' – 'Don't you know the mail's gone past already?' – 'Not already?' – 'Of course; it went past while you were sleeping.' – 'I wasn't sleeping. What an idea!' – 'Oh shut up, you're still half asleep.' – 'But I wasn't.' – 'Come on!'

We ran bunched more closely together, many of us linked hands, one's head could not be held high enough, for now the way was downhill. Someone whooped an Indian war cry, our legs galloped us as never before, the wind lifted our hips as we sprang. Nothing could have checked us; we were in such full stride that even in overtaking others we could fold our arms and look quietly around us.

At the bridge over the brook we came to a stop; those who had overrun it came back. The water below lapped against stones and roots as if it were not already late evening. There was no reason why one of us should not jump onto the parapet of the bridge.

From behind clumps of trees in the distance a railway train came past, all the carriages were lit up, the windowpanes were certainly let down. One of us began to sing a popular catch, but we all felt like singing. We sang much faster than the train was going, we waved our arms because our voices were not enough, our voices rushed together in an avalanche of sound that did us good. When one joins in song with others it is like being drawn on by a fish hook.

So we sang, the forest behind us, for the ears of the distant travellers. The grownups were still awake in the village, the mothers were making down the beds for the night.

Our time was up. I kissed the one next to me, reached hands to the three nearest, and began to run home, none called me back. At the first crossroads where they could no longer see me I turned off and ran by the field paths into the forest again. I was making for that city in the south of which it was said in our village: 'There you'll find queer folk! Just think, they never sleep!' 'And why not?' 'Because they never get tired.' 'And why not?' 'Because they're fools.' 'Don't fools get tired?' 'How could fools get tired!'

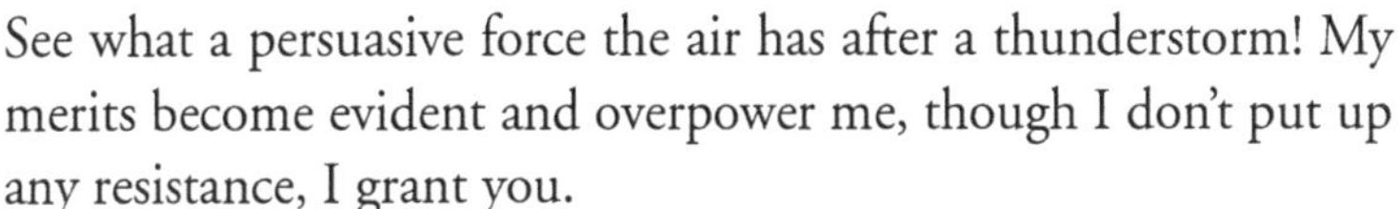

Story 11
THE WAY HOME

See what a persuasive force the air has after a thunderstorm! My merits become evident and overpower me, though I don't put up any resistance, I grant you.

I stride along and my tempo is the tempo of all my side of the street, of the whole street, of the whole quarter. Mine is the responsibility, and rightly so, for all the raps on doors or on the flat of a table, for all toasts drunk, for lovers in their beds, in the scaffolding of new buildings, pressed to each other against the house walls in dark alleys, or on the divans of a brothel.

I weigh my past against my future, but find both of them admirable, cannot give either the preference, and find nothing to grumble at save the injustice of providence that has so clearly favored me.

Only as I come into my room I feel a little meditative, without having met anything on the stairs worth meditating about. It doesn't help me much to open the window wide and hear music still playing in a garden.

Story 12

UNHAPPINESS

When it was becoming unbearable once toward evening in November and I ran along the narrow strip of carpet in my room as on a racetrack, shrank from the sight of the lit-up street, then turning to the interior of the room found a new goal in the depths of the looking glass and screamed aloud, to hear only my own scream which met no answer nor anything that could draw its force away, so that it rose up without check and could not stop even when it ceased being audible, the door in the wall opened toward me, how swiftly, because swiftness was needed and even the cart horses down below on the paving stones were rising in the air like horses driven wild in a battle, their throats bare to the enemy.

Like a small ghost a child blew in from the pitch dark corridor, where the lamp was not yet lit, and stood a tiptoe on a floor board that quivered imperceptibly. At once dazzled by the twilight in my room she made to cover her face quickly with her hands, but contented herself unexpectedly with a glance at the window, where the mounting vapor of the street lighting had at last settled under its cover of darkness behind the crossbars. With her right elbow she supported herself against the wall in the open doorway and let the draught from outside play along her ankles, her throat, and her temples.

I gave her a brief glance, then said 'Good day,' and took my jacket from the hood of the stove, since I didn't want to stand there half undressed. For a little while I let my mouth hang open, so that my agitation could find a way out. I had a bad taste in my mouth, my eyelashes were fluttering on my cheeks, in short this visit, though I had expected it, was the one thing needful.

The child was still standing by the wall on the same spot, she had pressed her right hand against the plaster and was quite taken up with finding, her cheeks all pink, that the whitewashed walls had a rough surface and chafed her finger tips. I said: 'Are you really looking for me? Isn't there some mistake? Nothing easier than to make a mistake in this big building. I'm called So-and-so and I live on the third floor. Am I the person you want to find?

'Hush, hush,' said the child over her shoulder, 'it's all right.'

'Then come farther into the room, I'd like to shut the door.'

'I've shut it this very minute. Don't bother. Just be easy in your mind.'

'It's no bother. But there's a lot of people living on this corridor, and I know them all, of course; most of them are coming back from work now; if they hear someone talking in a room, they simply think they have a right to open the door and see what's happening. They're just like that. They've turned their backs on their daily work and in their provisionally free evenings they're not going to be dictated to by anyone. Besides, you know that as well as I do. Let me shut the door.'

'Why, what's the matter with you? I don't mind if the whole house comes in. Anyhow, as I told you, I've already shut the door, do you think you're the only person who can shut doors? I've even turned the key in the lock.'

'That's all right then. I couldn't ask for more. You didn't need to turn the key, either. And now that you are here, make yourself comfortable. You are my guest. You can trust me entirely. Just make yourself at home and don't be afraid. I won't compel you either to stay or to go away. Do I have to tell you that? Do you know me so little?'

'No. You really didn't need to tell me that. What's more, you shouldn't have told me. I'm just a child; why stand on so much ceremony with me?'

'It's not so bad as that. A child, of course. But not so very small. You're quite big. If you were a young lady, you wouldn't dare to lock yourself so simply in a room with me.'

'We needn't worry about that. I just want to say: my knowing you so well isn't much protection to me, it only relieves you of the effort of keeping up pretenses before me. And yet you're paying me a compliment. Stop it, I beg you, do stop it. Anyhow, I don't know you everywhere and all the time, least of all in this darkness. It would be much better if you were to light up. No, perhaps not. At any rate I'll keep it in mind that you have been threatening me.'

'What? Am I supposed to have threatened you? But, look here. I'm so pleased that you've come at last. I say "at last" because it's already rather late. I can't understand why you've come so late. But it's possible that in the joy of seeing you I have been speaking at random and you took up my words in the wrong sense. I'll admit ten times over that I said something of the kind, I've made all kinds of threats, anything you like. Only no quarreling, for Heaven's sake! But how could you think of such a thing? How could you hurt me so? Why do you insist on spoiling this brief moment of your presence here? A stranger would be more obliging than you are.'

'That I can well believe; that's no great discovery. No stranger could come any nearer to you than I am already by nature. You know that, too, so why all this pathos? If you're only wanting to stage a comedy I'll go away immediately.'

'What? You have the impudence to tell me that? You make a little too bold. After all, it's my room you're in. It's my wall you're rubbing your fingers on like mad. My room, my wall! And besides, what you are saying is ridiculous as well as impudent. You say your nature forces you to speak to me like that. Is that so? Your nature forces you? That's kind of your nature. Your nature is mine, and if I feel friendly to you by nature, then you mustn't be anything else.'

'Is that friendly?'

'I'm speaking of earlier on.'

'Do you know how I'll be later on?'

'I don't know anything.'

And I went to the bed table and lit the candle on it. At that time I had neither gas nor electric light in my room. Then I sat for a while at the table till I got tired of it, put on my greatcoat, took my hat from the sofa, and blew out the candle. As I went out I tripped over the leg of a chair.

On the stairs I met one of the tenants from my floor.

'Going out again already, you rascal?' he asked, pausing with his legs firmly straddled over two steps.'

'What can I do?' I said, 'I've just had a ghost in my room.'

'You say that exactly as if you had just found a hair in your soup.'

'You're making a joke of it. But let me tell you, a ghost is a ghost.'

'How true. But what if one doesn't believe in ghosts at all?'

'Well, do you think I believe in ghosts? But how can my not believing help me?'

'Quite simply. You don't need to feel afraid if a ghost actually turns up.'

'Oh, that's only a secondary fear. The real fear is a fear of what caused the apparition. And that fear doesn't go away. I have it fairly powerfully inside me now.' Out of sheer nervousness I began to hunt through all my pockets.

'But since you weren't afraid of the ghost itself, you could easily have asked it how it came to be there.'

'Obviously you've never spoken to a ghost. One never gets straight information from them. It's just a hither and thither. These ghosts seem to be more dubious about their existence than we are, and no wonder, considering how frail they are.'

'But I've heard that one can fatten them up.'

'How well informed you are. It's quite true. But is anyone likely to do it?'

'Why not? If it were a feminine ghost, for instance,' said he, swinging onto the top step.

'Aha,' said I, 'but even then it's not worth while.'

I thought of something else. My neighbor was already so far up that in order to see me he had to bend over the well of the staircase. 'All the same,' I called up, 'if you steal my ghost from me all is over between us, forever.'

'Oh, I was only joking,' he said and drew his head back.

'That's all right,' said I, and now I really could have gone quietly for a walk. But because I felt so forlorn I preferred to go upstairs again and so went to bed.

Story 13

UNMASKING A CONFIDENCE TRICKSTER

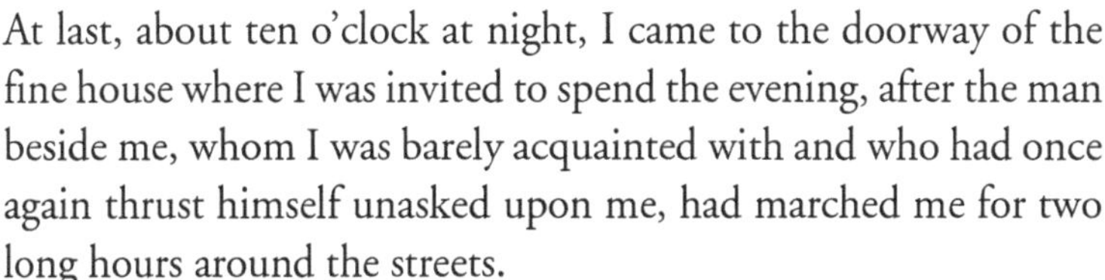

At last, about ten o'clock at night, I came to the doorway of the fine house where I was invited to spend the evening, after the man beside me, whom I was barely acquainted with and who had once again thrust himself unasked upon me, had marched me for two long hours around the streets.

'Well!' I said, and clapped my hands to show that I really had to bid him goodbye. I had already made several less explicit attempts to get rid of him. I was tired out. 'Are you going straight in?' he asked. I heard a sound in his mouth that was like the snapping of teeth. 'Yes.'

I had been invited out, I told him when I met him. But it was to enter a house where I longed to be that I had been invited, not to stand here at the street door looking past the ears of the man before me. Nor to fall silent with him, as if we were doomed to stay for a long time on this spot. And yet the houses around us at once took a share in our silence, and the darkness over them, all the way up to the stars. And the steps of invisible passers-by, which one could not take the trouble to elucidate, and the wind persistently buffeting the other side of the street, and a gramophone singing behind the closed windows of some room they all announced themselves in this silence, as if it were their own possession for the time past and to come.

And my companion subscribed to it in his own name and with a smile in mine too, stretched his right arm up along the wall and leaned his cheek upon it, shutting his eyes.

But I did not wait to see the end of that smile, for shame suddenly caught hold of me. It had needed that smile to let me know that the man was a confidence trickster, nothing else. And yet I had been months in the town and thought I knew all about confidence tricksters, how they came slinking out of side streets by night to meet us with outstretched hands like tavern keepers, how they haunted the advertisement pillars we stood beside, sliding around them as if playing hide-and-seek and spying on us with at least one eye, how they suddenly appeared on the curb of the pavement at cross-streets when we were hesitating! I understood them so well, they were the first acquaintances I had made in the town's small taverns, and to them I owed my first inkling of a ruthless hardness which I was now so conscious of, everywhere on earth, that I was even beginning to feel it in myself. How persistently they blocked our way, even when we had long shaken ourselves free, even when, that is, they had nothing more to hope for! How they refused to give up, to admit defeat, but kept shooting glances at us that even from a distance were still compelling! And the means they employed were always the same: they planted themselves before us, looking as large as possible, tried to hinder us from going where we purposed, offered us instead a habitation in their own bosoms, and when at last all our balked feelings rose in revolt they welcomed that like an embrace into which they threw themselves face foremost.

And it had taken me such a long time in this man's company to recognize the same old game. I rubbed my finger tips together to wipe away the disgrace.

My companion was still leaning there as before, still believing himself a successful trickster, and his self-complacency glowed pink on his free cheek.

'Caught in the act!' said I, tapping him lightly on the shoulder. Then I ran up the steps, and the disinterested devotion on the servants' faces in the hall delighted me like an unexpected treat. I looked at them all, one after another, while they took my greatcoat off and wiped my shoes clean.

With a deep breath of relief and straightening myself to my full height, I then entered the drawing room.

Story 14

ON THE TRAM

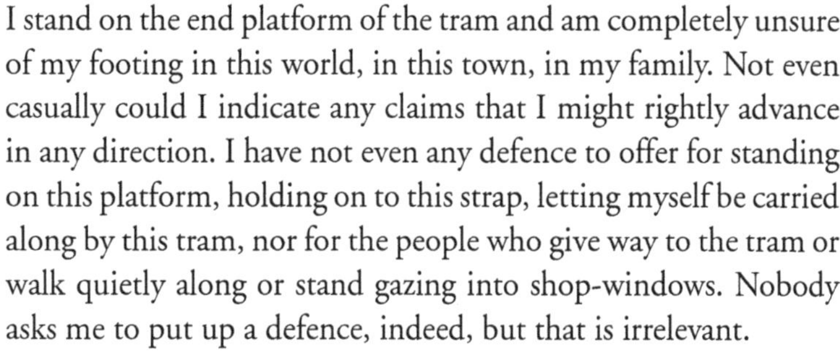

I stand on the end platform of the tram and am completely unsure of my footing in this world, in this town, in my family. Not even casually could I indicate any claims that I might rightly advance in any direction. I have not even any defence to offer for standing on this platform, holding on to this strap, letting myself be carried along by this tram, nor for the people who give way to the tram or walk quietly along or stand gazing into shop-windows. Nobody asks me to put up a defence, indeed, but that is irrelevant.

The tram approaches a stopping place and a girl takes up her position near the step, ready to alight. She is as distinct to me as if I had run my hands over her. She is dressed in black, the pleats of her skirt hang almost still, her blouse is tight and has a collar of white fine meshed lace, her left hand is braced flat against the side of the tram, the umbrella in her right hand rests on the second top step. Her face is brown, her nose, slightly pinched at the sides, has a broad round trip. She has a lot of brown hair and stray little tendrils on the right temple. Her small ear is close set, but since

I am near her I can see the whole ridge of the whorl of her right ear and the shadow at the root of it.

At that point I asked myself: How is it that she is not amazed at herself, that she keeps her lips closed and makes no such remark?

Story 15

IN THE PENAL COLONY

"It's a peculiar apparatus," said the Officer to the Traveller, gazing with a certain admiration at the device, with which he was, of course, thoroughly familiar. It appeared that the Traveller had responded to the invitation of the Commandant only out of politeness, when he had been asked to attend the execution of a soldier condemned for disobeying and insulting his superior. Of course, interest in the execution was not very high even in the penal colony itself. At least, here in the small, deep, sandy valley, closed in on all sides by barren slopes, apart from the Officer and the Traveller there were present only the Condemned, a vacant looking man with a broad mouth and dilapidated hair and face, and the Soldier, who held the heavy chain to which were connected the small chains which bound the Condemned Man by his feet and wrist bones, as well as by his neck, and which were also linked to each other by connecting chains. The Condemned Man, incidentally, had an expression of such dog like resignation that it looked as if one could set him free to roam around the slopes and would only have to whistle at the start of the execution for him to return.

The Traveller had little interest in the apparatus and walked back and forth behind the Condemned Man, almost visibly indifferent, while the Officer took care of the final preparations. Sometimes he crawled under the apparatus, which was built deep into the earth, and sometimes he climbed up a ladder to inspect the upper parts. These were really jobs which could have been left to a mechanic, but the Officer carried them out with great enthusiasm, maybe because he was particularly fond of this apparatus or maybe because there was some other reason why one could not trust the work to anyone else. "It's all ready now!" he finally cried and climbed back down the ladder. He was unusually tired, breathing with his mouth wide open, and he had pushed two fine lady's handkerchiefs under the collar of his uniform.

"These uniforms are really too heavy for the tropics," the Traveller said, instead of asking some questions about the apparatus, as the Officer had expected. "That's true," said the Officer. He washed the oil and grease from his dirty hands in a bucket of water standing ready, "but they mean home, and we don't want to lose our homeland." "Now, have a look at this apparatus," he added immediately, drying his hands with a towel and pointing to the device. "Up to this point I had to do some work by hand, but from now on the apparatus should work entirely on its own." The Traveller nodded and followed the Officer. The latter tried to protect himself against all eventualities by saying, "Of course, breakdowns do happen. I really hope none will occur today, but we must be prepared for it. The apparatus is supposed to keep going for twelve hours without interruption.

But if any breakdowns do occur, they'll only be very minor, and we'll deal with them right away."

“Don’t you want to sit down?” he asked finally, as he pulled out a chair from a pile of cane chairs and offered it to the Traveller. The latter could not refuse. He sat on the edge of the pit, into which he cast a fleeting glance. It was not very deep. On one side of the hole the piled earth was heaped up into a wall; on the other side stood the apparatus. “I don’t know,” the Officer said, “whether the Commandant has already explained the apparatus to you.” The Traveller made an vague gesture with his hand. That was good enough for the Officer, for now he could explain the apparatus himself.

“This apparatus,” he said, grasping a connecting rod and leaning against it, “is our previous Commandant’s invention. I also worked with him on the very first tests and took part in all the work right up to its completion. However, the credit for the invention belongs to him alone. Have you heard of our previous Commandant? No? Well, I’m not claiming too much when I say that the organization of the entire penal colony is his work. We, his friends, already knew at the time of his death that the administration of the colony was so self contained that even if his successor had a thousand new plans in mind, he would not be able to alter anything of the old plan, at least not for several years. And our prediction has held. The New Commandant has had to recognize that. It’s a shame that you didn’t know the previous Commandant!”

“However,” the Officer said, interrupting himself, “I’m chattering, and his apparatus stands here in front of us. As you see, it consists of three parts. With the passage of time certain popular names have been developed for each of these parts. The one underneath is called the Bed, the upper one is called the Inscriber, and here in the middle, this moving part is called the Harrow.” “The Harrow?” the Traveller asked. He had not been listening with full attention. The sun was excessively strong, trapped in the shadow less valley, and one could hardly collect one's thoughts. So the Officer appeared to him all the more admirable in his tight tunic weighed down with epaulettes and festooned with braid, ready to go on parade, as he explained the matter so eagerly and, while he was talking, adjusted screws here and there with a screwdriver.

The Soldier appeared to be in a state similar to the Traveller. He had wound the Condemned Man's chain around both his wrists and was supporting himself with his hand on his weapon, letting his head hang backward, not bothering about anything. The Traveller was not surprised at that, for the Officer spoke French, and clearly neither the Soldier nor the Condemned Man understood the language. So it was all the more striking that the Condemned Man, in spite of that, did what he could to follow the Officer's explanation.

With a sort of sleepy persistence he kept directing his gaze to the place where the Officer had just pointed, and when a question from the Traveller interrupted the Officer, the Condemned Man looked at the Traveller, too, just as the Officer was doing.

"Yes, the Harrow," said the Officer. "The name fits. The needles are arranged as in a harrow, and the whole thing is driven like a harrow, although it stays in one place and is, in principle, much more artistic. You'll understand in a moment. The condemned is laid out here on the Bed. First, I'll describe the apparatus and only then let the procedure go to work. That way you'll be able to follow it better. Also a sprocket in the Inscriber is excessively worn. It really squeaks. When it's in motion one can hardly make oneself understood. Unfortunately replacement parts are difficult to come by in this place. So, here is the Bed, as I said. The whole thing is completely covered with a layer of cotton wool, the purpose of which you'll find out in a moment. The condemned man is laid out on his stomach on the cotton wool—naked, of course. There are straps for the hands here, for the feet here, and for the throat here, to tie him in securely. At the head of the Bed here, where the man, as I have mentioned, first lies face down, is this small protruding lump of felt, which can easily be adjusted so that it presses right into the man's mouth. Its purpose is to prevent him screaming and biting his tongue to pieces. Of course, the man has to let the felt in his mouth—otherwise the straps around his throat would break his neck." "That's cotton wool?" asked the Traveller and bent down. "Yes, it is," said the Officer smiling, "feel it for yourself."

He took the Traveller's hand and led him over to the Bed. "It's a specially prepared cotton wool. That's why it looks so unrecognizable. I'll get around to mentioning its purpose in a moment." The Traveller was already being won over a little to the apparatus. With his hand over his eyes to protect them from the sun, he looked up at the height of the apparatus. It was a massive construction. The Bed and the Inscriber were the same size and looked like two dark chests. The Inscriber was set about two metres above the Bed, and the two were joined together at the corners by four brass rods, which almost reflected the sun. The Harrow hung between the chests on a band of steel.

The Officer had hardly noticed the earlier indifference of the Traveller, but he did have a sense now of how the latter's interest was being aroused for the first time. So he paused in his explanation in order to allow the Traveller time to observe the apparatus undisturbed. The Condemned Man imitated the Traveller, but since he could not put his hand over his eyes, he blinked upward with his eyes uncovered.

"So now the man is lying down," said the Traveller. He leaned back in his chair and crossed his legs.

"Yes," said the Officer, pushing his cap back a little and running his hand over his hot face. "Now, listen.

Both the Bed and the Inscriber have their own electric batteries. The Bed needs them for itself, and the Inscriber for the Harrow. As soon as the man is strapped in securely, the Bed is set in motion. It quivers with tiny, very rapid oscillations from side to side and up and down simultaneously. You will have seen similar devices in mental hospitals. Only with our Bed all movements are precisely calibrated, for they must be meticulously coordinated with the movements of the Harrow. But it's the Harrow which has the job of actually carrying out the sentence."

"What is the sentence?" the Traveller asked. "You don't even know that?" asked the Officer in astonishment and bit his lip. "Forgive me if my explanations are perhaps confused. I really do beg your pardon. Previously it was the Commandant's habit to provide such explanations. But the New Commandant has excused himself from this honourable duty. The fact that with such an eminent visitor"—the Traveller tried to deflect the honour with both hands, but the Officer insisted on the expression—"that with such an eminent visitor he didn't even once make him aware of the form of our sentencing is yet again something new, which . . . ." He had a curse on his lips, but controlled himself and said merely: "I was not informed about it. It's not my fault. In any case, I am certainly the person best able to explain our style of sentencing, for here I am carrying"—he patted his breast pocket—"the relevant diagrams drawn by the previous Commandant."

"Diagrams made by the Commandant himself?" asked the Traveller. "Then was he in his own person a combination of everything? Was he soldier, judge, engineer, chemist, and draftsman?"

"He was indeed," said the Officer, nodding his head with a fixed and thoughtful expression. Then he looked at his hands, examining them. They didn't seem to him clean enough to handle the diagrams. So he went to the bucket and washed them again.

Then he pulled out a small leather folder and said, "Our sentence does not sound severe. The law which a condemned man has violated is inscribed on his body with the Harrow. This Condemned Man, for example," and the Officer pointed to the man, "will have inscribed on his body, 'Honour your superiors.'"

The Traveller had a quick look at the man. When the Officer was pointing at him, the man kept his head down and appeared to be directing all his energy into listening in order to learn something. But the movements of his thick pouting lips showed clearly that he was incapable of understanding anything. The Traveller wanted to raise various questions, but after looking at the Condemned Man he merely asked, "Does he know his sentence?" "No," said the Officer. He wished to get on with his explanation right away, but the Traveller interrupted him: "He doesn't know his own sentence?" "No," said the Officer once more.

He then paused for a moment, as if he was asking the Traveller for a more detailed reason for his question, and said, "It would be useless to give him that information. He experiences it on his own body." The Traveller really wanted to keep quiet at this point, but he felt how the Condemned Man was gazing at him—he seemed to be asking whether he could approve of the process the Officer had described. So the Traveller, who had up to this point been leaning back, bent forward again and kept up his questions, "But does he nonetheless have some general idea that he's been condemned?" "Not that either," said the Officer, and he smiled at the Traveller, as if he was still waiting for some strange revelations from him. "No?" said the Traveller, wiping his forehead, "Then does the man also not yet know how his defence was received?" "He has had no opportunity to defend himself," said the Officer and looked away, as if he was talking to himself and wished not to embarrass the Traveller with an explanation of matters so self evident to him. "But he must have had a chance to defend himself," said the Traveller and stood up from his chair.

The Officer recognized that he was in danger of having his explanation of the apparatus held up for a long time. So he went to the Traveller, took him by the arm, pointed with his hand at the Condemned Man, who stood there stiffly now that the attention was so clearly directed at him—the Soldier was also pulling on his chain—and said, "The matter stands like this. Here in the penal colony I have been appointed judge. In spite of my youth. For I stood at the side of our Old Commandant in all matters of punishment, and I also know the most about the apparatus. The basic principle I use for my decisions is this: Guilt is always beyond a doubt. Other courts could not follow this principle, for they are made up of many heads and, in addition, have even higher courts above them. But that is not the case here, or at least it was not that way with the previous Commandant. It's true the New Commandant has already shown a desire to get mixed up in my court, but I've succeeded so far in fending him off. And I'll continue to be successful. You want this case explained. It's simple—just like all of them. This morning a captain laid a charge that this man, who is assigned to him as a servant and who sleeps before his door, had been sleeping on duty. For his task is to stand up every time the clock strikes the hour and salute in front of the captain's door. That's certainly not a difficult duty—and it's necessary, since he is supposed to remain fresh both for guarding and for service. Yesterday night the captain wanted to check whether his servant was fulfilling his duty. He opened the door on the stroke of two and found him curled up asleep. He got his horsewhip and hit him across the face. Now, instead of standing up and begging for forgiveness, the man grabbed his master by the legs, shook him, and cried out, 'Throw away that whip or I'll eat you up.' Those are the facts.

The captain came to me an hour ago. I wrote up his statement and right after that the sentence. Then I had the man chained up. It was all very simple. If I had first summoned the man and interrogated him, the result would have been confusion. He would have lied, and if I had been successful in refuting his lies, he would have replaced them with new lies, and so forth. But now I have him, and I won't release him again. Now, does that clarify everything? But time is passing. We should be starting the execution, and I haven't finished explaining the apparatus yet."

He urged the Traveller to sit down in his chair, moved to the apparatus again, and started, "As you see, the shape of the Harrow corresponds to the shape of a man. This is the harrow for the upper body, and here are the harrows for the legs. This small cutter is the only one designated for the head. Is that clear to you?" He leaned forward to the Traveller in a friendly way, ready to give the most comprehensive explanation.

The Traveller looked at the Harrow with a wrinkled frown. The information about the judicial procedures had not satisfied him. However, he had to tell himself that here it was a matter of a penal colony, that in this place special regulations were necessary, and that one had to give precedence to military measures right down to the last detail. Beyond that, however, he had some hopes in the New Commandant, who obviously, although slowly, was intending to introduce a new procedure which the limited understanding of this Officer could not cope with.

Following this train of thought, the Traveller asked, "Will the Commandant be present at the execution?" "That is not certain," said the Officer, embarrassingly affected by the sudden question, and his friendly expression made a grimace. "That's why we need to hurry up. As much as I regret the fact, I'll have to make my explanation even shorter. But tomorrow, once the apparatus is clean again—the fact that it gets so very dirty is its only fault—I could add a detailed explanation. So now, only the most important things. When the man is lying on the Bed and it starts quivering, the Harrow sinks onto the body. It positions itself automatically in such a way that it touches the body only lightly with the needle tips. Once the machine is set in this position, this steel cable tightens up into a rod. And now the performance begins. Someone who is not an initiate sees no external difference among the punishments. The Harrow seems to do its work uniformly. As it quivers, it sticks the tips of its needles into the body, which is also vibrating from the movement of the bed. Now, to enable someone to check on how the sentence is being carried out, the Harrow is made of glass. That gave rise to certain technical difficulties with fastening the needles securely, but after several attempts we were successful. We didn't spare any efforts.

And now, as the inscription is made on the body, everyone can see through the glass. Don't you want to come closer and see the needles for yourself."

The Traveller stood slowly, moved up, and bent over the Harrow. "You see," the Officer said, "two sorts of needles in a multiple arrangement. Each long needle has a short one next to it. The long one inscribes, and the short one squirts water out to wash away the blood and keep the inscription always clear. The bloody water is then channelled here in small grooves and finally flows into these main gutters, and the outlet pipe takes it to the pit." The Officer pointed with his finger to the exact path which the bloody water had to take. As he began to demonstrate with both hands at the mouth of the outlet pipe, in order to make his account as clear as possible, the Traveller raised his head and, feeling behind him with his hand, wanted to return to his chair. Then he saw to his horror that the Condemned Man had also, like him, accepted the Officer's invitation to inspect the arrangement of the Harrow up close. He had pulled the sleeping Soldier holding the chain a little forward and was also bending over the glass. One could see how with a confused gaze he also was looking for what the two gentlemen had just observed, but how he didn't succeed because he lacked the explanation. He leaned forward this way and that. He kept running his eyes over the glass again and again. The Traveller wanted to push him back, for what he was doing was probably punishable. But the Officer held the Traveller firmly with one hand, and with the other he took a lump of earth from the wall and threw it at the Soldier. The latter opened his eyes with a start, saw what the Condemned Man had dared to do, let his weapon fall, braced his heels in the earth, and pulled the Condemned Man back, so that he immediately collapsed. The Soldier looked down at him, as he writhed around, making his chain clink. "Stand him up," cried the Officer, for he noticed that the Condemned Man was distracting the Traveller too much. The latter was even leaning out away from the Harrow, without paying any attention to it, wanting to find out what was happening to the Condemned Man. "Handle him carefully," the Officer yelled again. He ran around the apparatus, personally grabbed the Condemned Man under the armpits and, with the help of the Soldier, stood the man, whose feet kept slipping, upright.

"Now I know all about it," said the Traveller, as the Officer turned back to him again. "Except the most important thing," said the latter, grabbing the Traveller by the arm and pointing up high. "There in the Inscriber is the mechanism which determines the movement of the Harrow, and this mechanism is arranged according to the diagram on which the sentence is set down. I still use the diagrams of the previous Commandant. Here they are." He pulled some pages out of the leather folder. "Unfortunately I can't hand them to you.

They are the most cherished thing I possess. Sit down, and I'll show you them from this distance. Then you'll be able to see it all well." He showed the first sheet. The Traveller would have been happy to say something appreciative, but all he saw was a labyrinthine series of lines, criss-crossing each other in all sort of ways. These covered the paper so thickly that only with difficulty could one make out the white spaces in between. "Read it," said the Officer. "I can't," said the Traveller. "But it's clear," said the Officer." "It's very elaborate," said the Traveller evasively, "but I can't decipher it."

"Yes," said the Officer, smiling and putting the folder back again, "it's not calligraphy for school children. One has to read it a long time. You too will finally understand it clearly. Of course, it has to be a script that isn't simple. You see, it's not supposed to kill right away, but on average over a period of twelve hours. The turning point is set for the sixth hour. There must also be many, many embellishments surrounding the basic script. The essential script moves around the body only in a narrow belt. The rest of the body is reserved for decoration. Can you now appreciate the work of the Harrow and the whole apparatus? Just look at it!" He jumped up the ladder, turned a wheel, and called down, "Watch out—move to the side!" Everything started moving. If the wheel had not squeaked, it would have been marvellous. The Officer threatened the wheel with his fist, as if he was surprised by the disturbance it created. Then he spread his arms, apologizing to the Traveller, and quickly clambered down, in order to observe the operation of the apparatus from below.

Something was still not working properly, something only he noticed. He clambered up again and reached with both hands into the inside of the Inscriber. Then, in order to descend more quickly, instead of using the ladder, he slid down on one of the poles and, to make himself understandable through the noise, strained his voice to the limit as he yelled in the Traveller's ear, "Do you understand the process? The Harrow is starting to write.

When it's finished with the first part of the script on the man's back, the layer of cotton wool rolls and turns the body slowly onto its side to give the Harrow a new area. Meanwhile those parts lacerated by the inscription are lying on the cotton wool which, because it has been specially treated, immediately stops the bleeding and prepares the script for a further deepening. Here, as the body continues to rotate, prongs on the edge of the Harrow then pull the cotton wool from the wounds, throw it into the pit, and the Harrow goes to work again. In this way it keeps making the inscription deeper for twelve hours. For the first six hours the condemned man goes on living almost as before. He suffers nothing but pain. After two hours, the felt is removed, for at that point the man has no more energy for screaming.

Here at the head of the Bed warm rice pudding is put in this electrically heated bowl. From this the man, if he feels like it, can help himself to what he can lap up with his tongue. No one passes up this opportunity. I don't know of a single one, and I have had a lot of experience. He first loses his pleasure in eating around the sixth hour. I usually kneel down at this point and observe the phenomenon. The man rarely swallows the last bit. He turns it around in his mouth and spits it into the pit. When he does that, I have to lean aside or else he'll get me in the face. But how quiet the man becomes around the sixth hour! The most stupid of them begin to understand. It starts around the eyes and spreads out from there. A look that could tempt one to lie down under the Harrow. Nothing else happens. The man simply begins to decipher the inscription. He pursues his lips, as if he is listening. You've seen that it's not easy to figure out the inscription with your eyes, but our man deciphers it with his wounds. True, it takes a lot of work. It requires six hours to complete. But then the Harrow spits him right out and throws him into the pit, where he splashes down into the bloody water and cotton wool. Then the judgment is over, and we, the Soldier and I, quickly bury him."

The Traveller had learned his ear towards the Officer and, with his hands in his coat pockets, was observing the machine at work. The Condemned Man was also watching, but without understanding. He bent forward a little and followed the moving needles, as the Soldier, after a signal from the Officer, cut through his shirt and trousers with a knife from the back, so that they fell off the Condemned Man. He wanted to grab the falling garments to cover his bare flesh, but the Soldier held him up and shook the last rags from him. The Officer turned the machine off, and in the silence which then ensued the Condemned Man was laid out under the Harrow. The chains were taken off and the straps fastened in their place. For the Condemned Man it seemed at first glance to signify almost a relief. And now the Harrow sunk down a stage lower, for the Condemned was a thin man. As the needle tips touched him, a shudder went over his skin. While the Soldier was busy with the right hand, the Condemned Man stretched out his left, with no sense of its direction. But it was pointing to where the Traveller was standing. The Officer kept looking at the Traveller from the side, without taking his eyes off him, as if he was trying to read from his face the impression he was getting of the execution, which he had now explained to him, at least superficially.

The strap meant to hold the wrist ripped off. The Soldier probably had pulled on it too hard. The Soldier showed the Officer the torn off piece of strap, wanting him to help. So the Officer went over to him and said, with his face turned towards the Traveller, "The machine is very complicated.

Now and then something has to tear or break. One shouldn't let that detract from one's overall opinion. Anyway, we have an immediate replacement for the strap. I'll use a chain—even though that will affect the sensitivity of the movements for the right arm." And while he put the chain in place, he kept talking, "Our resources for maintaining the machine are very limited at the moment. Under the previous Commandant, I had free access to a cash box specially set aside for this purpose. There was a store room here in which all possible replacement parts were kept. I admit I made almost extravagant use of it. I mean earlier, not now, as the New Commandant claims. For him everything serves only as a pretext to fight against the old arrangements. Now he keeps the cash box for machinery under his own control, and if I ask him for a new strap, he demands the torn one as a piece of evidence, the new one doesn't arrive for ten days, and it's an inferior brand, of not much use to me. But how I am supposed to get the machine to work in the meantime without a strap—no one's concerned about that."

The Traveller was thinking: it is always questionable to intervene decisively in strange circumstances. He was neither a citizen of the penal colony nor a citizen of the state to which it belonged. If he wanted to condemn the execution or even hinder it, people could say to him: You are a foreigner—keep quiet. He would have nothing in response to that, but could only add that he did not understand what he was doing on this occasion, for the purpose of his travelling was merely to observe and not to alter other people's judicial systems in any way. True, at this point the way things were turning out it was very tempting. The injustice of the process and the inhumanity of the execution were beyond doubt. No one could assume that the Traveller was acting out of any sense of his own self interest, for the Condemned Man was a stranger to him, not a countryman and not someone who invited sympathy in any way. The Traveller himself had letters of reference from high officials and had been welcomed here with great courtesy. The fact that he had been invited to this execution even seemed to indicate that people were asking for his judgment of this trial. This was all the more likely since the Commandant, as he had now heard only too clearly, was no supporter of this process and maintained an almost hostile relationship with the Officer.

Then the Traveller heard a cry of rage from the Officer. He had just shoved the stub of felt in the Condemned Man's mouth, not without difficulty, when the Condemned Man, overcome by an irresistible nausea, shut his eyes and threw up. The Officer quickly yanked him up off the stump and wanted to turn his head aside toward the pit. But it was too late. The vomit was already flowing down onto the machine. "This is all the Commandant's fault!" cried the Officer and mindlessly rattled the brass rods at the front.

"My machine's as filthy as a pigsty." With trembling hands he showed the Traveller what had happened. "Haven't I spent hours trying to make the Commandant understand that a day before the execution there should be no more food served. But the new lenient administration has a different opinion. Before the man is led away, the Commandant's women cram sugary things down his throat. His whole life he's fed himself on stinking fish, and now he has to eat sweets! But that would be all right—I'd have no objections—but why don't they get a new felt, the way I've been asking him for three months now? How can anyone take this felt into his mouth without feeling disgusted—something that a hundred man have sucked and bitten on it as they were dying?"

The Condemned Man had laid his head down and appeared peaceful. The Soldier was busy cleaning up the machine with the Condemned Man's shirt. The Officer went up to the Traveller, who, feeling some premonition, took a step backwards. But the Officer grasped him by the hand and pulled him aside. "I want to speak a few words to you in confidence," he said.

"May I do that?" "Of course," said the Traveller and listened with his eyes lowered.

"This process and execution, which you now have an opportunity to admire, have no more open supporters in our colony. I am its only defender, just as I am the single advocate for the legacy of the Old Commandant. I can no longer think about a more extensive organization of the process—I'm using all my powers to maintain what there is at present. When the Old Commandant was alive, the colony was full of his supporters. I have something of the Old Commandant's persuasiveness, but I completely lack his power, and as a result the supporters have gone into hiding. There are still a lot of them, but no one admits to it. If you go into a tea house today—that is to say, on a day of execution—and keep your ears open, perhaps you'll hear nothing but ambiguous remarks. They are all supporters, but under the present Commandant, considering his present views, they are totally useless to me. And now I'm asking you: Should such a life's work," he pointed to the machine, "come to nothing because of this Commandant and the women influencing him? Should people let that happen? Even if one is a foreigner and on our island only for a couple of days? But there's no time to lose. People are already preparing something against my judicial proceedings. Discussions are already taking place in the Commandant's headquarters, to which I am not invited. Even your visit today seems to me typical of the whole situation. People are cowards and send you out—a foreigner. You should have seen the executions in earlier days! The entire valley was overflowing with people, even a day before the execution. They all came merely to watch. Early in the morning the Commandant appeared with his women. Fanfares woke up the entire campsite. I delivered the news that everything was ready.

The whole society—and every high official had to attend—arranged itself around the machine. This pile of cane chairs is a sorry left over from that time. The machine was freshly cleaned and glowed. For almost every execution I had new replacement parts. In front of hundreds of eyes—all the spectators stood on tip toe right up to the hills there—the condemned man was laid down under the Harrow by the Commandant himself. What nowadays has to be done by a common soldier was then my work as the senior judge, and it was an honour for me. And then the execution began! No discordant note disturbed the work of the machine. Many people did not look any more at all, but lay down with closed eyes in the sand. They all knew: now justice was being carried out. In the silence people heard nothing but the groans of the condemned man, muffled by the felt. These days the machine no longer manages to squeeze a strong groan out of the condemned man—something the felt is not capable of smothering. But back then the needles which made the inscription dripped a caustic liquid which we are not permitted to use any more today. Well, then came the sixth hour. It was impossible to grant all the requests people made to be allowed to watch from up close. The Commandant, in his wisdom, arranged that the children should be taken care of before all the rest. Naturally, I was always allowed to stand close by, because of my official position. Often I crouched down there with two small children in my arms, on my right and left. How we all took in the expression of transfiguration on the martyred face! How we held our cheeks in the glow of this justice, finally attained and already passing away! What times we had, my friend!"

The Officer had obviously forgotten who was standing in front of him. He had put his arm around the Traveller and laid his head on his shoulder. The Traveller was extremely embarrassed. Impatiently he looked away over the Officer's head. The Soldier had ended his task of cleaning and had just shaken some rice pudding into the bowl from a tin. No sooner had the Condemned Man, who seemed to have fully recovered already, noticed this than his tongue began to lick at the pudding. The Soldier kept pushing him away, for the pudding was probably meant for a later time, but in any case it was not proper for the Soldier to reach in and grab some food with his dirty hands and eat it in front of the famished Condemned Man.

The Officer quickly collected himself. "I didn't want to upset you in any way," he said. "I know it is impossible to make someone understand those days now. Besides, the machine still works and operates on its own. It operates on its own even when it is standing alone in this valley. And at the end, the body still keeps falling in that incredibly soft flight into the pit, even if hundreds of people are not gathered like flies around the hole the way they used to be.

Back then we had to erect a strong railing around the pit. It was pulled out long ago."

The Traveller wanted to turn his face away from the Officer and looked aimlessly around him. The Officer thought he was looking at the wasteland of the valley. So he grabbed his hands, turned him around in order to catch his gaze, and asked, "Do you see the shame of it?"

But the Traveller said nothing. The Officer left him alone for a while. With his legs apart and his hands on his hips, the Officer stood still and looked at the ground. Then he smiled at the Traveller cheerfully and said, "Yesterday I was nearby when the Commandant invited you. I heard the invitation. I know the Commandant. I understood right away what he intended with his invitation. Although his power might be sufficiently great to take action against me, he doesn't yet dare to. But my guess is that with you he is exposing me to the judgment of a respected foreigner. He calculates things with care. You are now in your second day on the island. You didn't know the Old Commandant and his way of thinking. You are trapped in a European way of seeing things. Perhaps you are fundamentally opposed to the death penalty in general and to this kind of mechanical style of execution in particular. Moreover, you see how the execution is a sad procedure, without any public participation, using a partially damaged machine. Now, if we take all this together (so the Commandant thinks) surely one could easily imagine that that you would not consider my procedure proper? And if you didn't consider it right, you wouldn't keep quiet about it—I'm still speaking the mind of the Commandant—for you no doubt have faith that your tried-and-true convictions are correct. It's true that you have seen many peculiar things among many peoples and have learned to respect them. Thus, you will probably not speak out against the procedure with your full power, as you would perhaps in your own homeland. But the Commandant doesn't really need that. A casual word, merely a careless remark, is enough. It doesn't have to match your convictions at all, so long as it corresponds to his wishes. I'm certain he will use all his shrewdness to interrogate you. And his women will sit around in a circle and perk up their ears. You will say something like, 'Among us the judicial procedures are different,' or 'With us the accused is questioned before the verdict,' or 'We had torture only in the Middle Ages.' For you these observations appear as correct as they are self evident—innocent remarks which do not impugn my procedure. But how will the Commandant take them? I see him, our excellent Commandant—the way he immediately pushes his stool aside and hurries out to the balcony—I see his women, how they stream after him. I hear his voice—the women call it a thunder voice.

And now he's speaking: 'A great Western explorer who has been commissioned to inspect judicial procedures in all countries has just said that our process based on old customs is inhuman. After the verdict of such a personality it is, of course, no longer possible for me to tolerate this procedure. So from this day on I am ordering... and so forth.' You want to intervene—you didn't say what he is reporting—you didn't call my procedure inhuman; by contrast, in keeping with your deep insight, you consider it most humane and most worthy of human beings. You also admire this machinery. But it is too late. You don't even go onto the balcony, which is already filled with women. You want to attract attention. You want to cry out. But a lady's hand is covering your mouth, and I and the Old Commandant's work are lost."

The Traveller had to suppress a smile. So the work which he had considered so difficult was easy. He said evasively, "You're exaggerating my influence. The Commandant has read my letters of recommendation. He knows that I am no expert in judicial processes. If I were to express an opinion, it would be that of a lay person, no more significant than the opinion of anyone else, and in any case far less significant than the opinion of the Commandant, who, as I understand it, has very extensive powers in this penal colony. If his views of this procedure are as definite as you think they are, then I'm afraid the time has come for this procedure to end, without any need for my humble opinion."

Did the Officer understand by now? No, he did not yet get it. He shook his head vigorously, briefly looked back at the Condemned Man and the Soldier, who both flinched and stopped eating the rice, went up really close up to the Traveller, without looking into his face, but gazing at parts of his jacket, and said more gently than before: "You don't know the Commandant. Where he and all of us are concerned you are—forgive the expression—to a certain extent innocent. Your influence, believe me, cannot be overestimated. In fact, I was blissfully happy when I heard that you were to be present at the execution by yourself.

This order of the Commandant was aimed at me, but now I'll turn it to my advantage. Without being distracted by false insinuations and disparaging looks—which could not have been avoided with a greater number of participants at the execution—you have listened to my explanation, looked at the machine, and are now about to view the execution. Your verdict is no doubt already fixed. If some small uncertainties remain, witnessing the execution will remove them. And now I'm asking you—help me with the Commandant!"

The Traveller did not let him go on talking. "How can I do that," he cried. "It's totally impossible. I can help you as little as I can harm you."

"You could do it," said the Officer. With some apprehension the Traveller observed that the Officer was clenching his fists. "You could do it," repeated the Officer, even more emphatically. "I have a plan which must succeed. You think your influence is insufficient. I know it will be enough.

But assuming you're right, doesn't saving this whole procedure require one to try even those methods which may be inadequate? So listen to my plan. To carry it out, it's necessary, above all, for you to keep as quiet as possible today in the colony about your verdict on this procedure. Unless someone asks you directly, you should not express any view whatsoever. But what you do say must be short and vague. People should notice that it's difficult for you to speak about the subject, that you feel bitter, that, if you were to speak openly, you'd have to burst out cursing on the spot. I'm not asking you to lie, not at all. You should give only brief answers—something like, 'Yes, I've seen the execution' or 'Yes, I've heard the full explanation.' That's all—nothing further. For that will be enough of an indication for people to observe in you a certain bitterness, even if that's not what the Commandant will think. Naturally, he will completely misunderstand the issue and interpret it in his own way. My plan is based on that. Tomorrow a large meeting of all the higher administrative officials takes place at headquarters under the chairmanship of the Commandant. He, of course, understands how to turn such a meeting into a spectacle. A gallery has been built, which is always full of spectators. I'm compelled to take part in the discussions, though they fill me with disgust. In any case, you will certainly be invited to the meeting. If you follow my plan today and behave accordingly, the invitation will become an emphatic request. But should you for some inexplicable reason still not be invited, you must make sure you request an invitation. Then you'll receive one without question. Now, tomorrow you are sitting with the women in the Commandant's box. With frequent upward glances he reassures himself that you are there. After various trivial and ridiculous agenda items designed for the spectators—mostly harbour construction, always harbour construction—the judicial process comes up for discussion. If it's not raised by the Commandant himself or does not occur soon enough, I'll make sure that it comes up. I'll stand up and report on today's execution. Really briefly—just an announcement. Such a report is not really customary; however, I'll do it, nonetheless. The Commandant thanks me, as always, with a friendly smile. And now he cannot restrain himself. He seizes this excellent opportunity. 'The report of the execution,' he'll say, or something like that, 'has just been given. I would like to add to this report only the fact that this particular execution was attended by the great explorer whose visit confers such extraordinary honour on our colony, as you all know. Even the significance of our meeting today has been increased by his presence.

Should we not now ask this great explorer for his appraisal of the execution based on old customs and of the process which preceded it?' Of course, there is the noise of applause everywhere, universal agreement. And I'm louder than anyone. The Commandant bows before you and says, 'Then in everyone's name, I'm putting the question to you.' And now you step up to the railing. Place your hands where everyone can see them. Otherwise the ladies will grab them and play with your fingers. And now finally come your remarks. I don't know how I'll bear the tension up to then. In your speech you mustn't hold back. Let truth resound. Lean over the railing and shout it out—yes, yes, roar your opinion at the Commandant, your unshakeable opinion. But perhaps you don't want to do that. It doesn't suit your character. Perhaps in your country people behave differently in such situations. That's all right. That's perfectly satisfactory. Don't stand up at all. Just say a couple of words. Whisper them so that only the officials underneath you can just hear them. That's enough. You don't even have to say anything at all about the lack of attendance at the execution or about the squeaky wheel, the torn strap, the disgusting felt. No. I'll take over all further details, and, believe me, if my speech doesn't chase him out of the room, it will force him to his knees, so he'll have to admit it: 'Old Commandant, I bow down before you.' That's my plan. Do you want to help me carry it out? But, of course, you want to. More than that—you have to."

And the Officer gripped the Traveller by both arms and looked at him, breathing heavily into his face. He had yelled the last sentences so loudly that even the Soldier and the Condemned Man were paying attention. Although they couldn't understand a thing, they stopped eating and looked over at the Traveller, still chewing.

From the start the Traveller had had no doubts about the answer he must give. He had experienced too much in his life to be able to waver here. Basically he was honest and unafraid. Still, with the Soldier and the Condemned Man looking at him, he hesitated a moment. But finally he said, as he had to, "No."

The Officer's eyes blinked several times, but he did not take his eyes off the Traveller. "Would you like an explanation," asked the Traveller. The Officer nodded dumbly. "I am opposed to this procedure," said the Traveller. "Even before you took me into your confidence—and, of course, I will never abuse your confidence under any circumstances—I was already thinking about whether I was entitled to intervene against this procedure and whether my intervention could have the smallest chance of success. And if that was the case, it was clear to me whom I had to turn to first of all—naturally, to the Commandant. You clarified the issue for me even more, but without reinforcing my decision in any way—quite the reverse. I find your conviction genuinely moving, even if it cannot deter me.

The Officer remained quiet, turned toward the machine, grabbed one of the brass rods, and then, leaning back a little, looked up at the Inscriber, as if he was checking that everything was in order. The Soldier and the Condemned Man seemed to have made friends with each other. The Condemned Man was making signs to the Soldier, although, given the tight straps on him, this was difficult for him to do. The Soldier was leaning into him. The Condemned Man whispered something to him, and the Soldier nodded. The Traveller went over to the Officer and said, "You don't yet know what I'll do. Yes, I will tell the Commandant my opinion of the procedure—not in a meeting, but in private. In addition, I won't stay here long enough to be able to get called in to some meeting or other. Early tomorrow morning I leave, or at least I go on board ship."

It did not look as if the Officer had been listening. "So the process has not convinced you," he said to himself, smiling the way an old man smiles over the silliness of a child, concealing his own true thoughts behind that smile.

"Well then, it's time," he said finally and suddenly looked at the Traveller with bright eyes which contained some sort of demand, some appeal for participation. "Time for what?" asked the Traveller uneasily. But there was no answer.

"You are free," the Officer told the Condemned Man in his own language. At first the man did not believe him. "You are free now," said the Officer. For the first time the face of the Condemned Man showed signs of real life. Was it the truth? Was it only the Officer's mood, which could change? Had the foreign Traveller brought him a reprieve? What was it? That is what the man's face seemed to be asking. But not for long. Whatever the case might be, if he could he wanted to be truly free, and he began to shake back and forth, as much as the Harrow permitted.

"You're tearing my straps," cried the Officer. "Be still! We'll undo them right away." And, giving a signal to the Soldier, he set to work with him. The Condemned Man said nothing and smiled slightly to himself. He turned his face to the Officer and then to the Soldier and then back again, without ignoring the Traveller.

"Pull him out," the Officer ordered the Soldier. This process required a certain amount of care because of the Harrow. The Condemned Man already had a few small wounds on his back, thanks to his own impatience.

From this point on, however, the Officer paid him hardly any attention. He went up to the Traveller, pulled out the small leather folder once more, leafed through it, finally found the sheet he was looking for, and showed it to the Traveller. "Read that," he said. "I can't," said the Traveller. "I've already told you I can't read these pages." "But take a close look at the page," said the Officer and moved up right next to the Traveller in order to read with him. When that didn't help, he raised his little finger high up over the paper, as if the page must not be touched under any circumstances, so that using this he might make the task of reading easier for the Traveller.

The Traveller also made an effort so that at least he could satisfy the Officer, but it was impossible for him. Then the Officer began to spell out the inscription and then read out once again the joined up letters. "'Be just!' it states," he said. "Now you can read it." The Traveller bent so low over the paper that the Officer, afraid that he might touch it, moved it further away. The Traveller didn't say anything more, but it was clear that he was still unable to read anything. "'Be just!' it says," the Officer remarked once again.

"That could be," said the Traveller. "I do believe that's written there." "Good," said the Officer, at least partially satisfied. He climbed up the ladder, holding the paper. With great care he set the page in the Inscriber and appeared to rotate the gear mechanism completely around. This was very tiring work. It must have required him to deal with extremely small wheels. He had to inspect the gears so closely that sometimes his head disappeared completely into the Inscriber.

The Traveller followed this work from below without looking away. His neck grew stiff, and his eyes found the sunlight pouring down from the sky painful. The Soldier and the Condemned Man were keeping each other busy. With the tip of his bayonet the Soldier pulled out the Condemned Man's shirt and trousers which were lying in the hole. The shirt was horribly dirty, and the Condemned Man washed it in the bucket of water. When he was putting on his shirt and trousers, the Soldier and the Condemned Man had to laugh out loud, for the pieces of clothing were cut in two up the back. Perhaps the Condemned Man thought that it was his duty to amuse the Soldier. In his ripped up clothes he circled around the Soldier, who crouched down on the ground, laughed, and slapped his knees. But they restrained themselves out of consideration for the two gentlemen present.

When the Officer was finally finished up on the machine, with a smile he looked over the whole thing and all its parts once more, and this time closed the cover of the Inscriber, which had been open up to this point. He climbed down, looked into the hole and then at the Condemned Man, observed with satisfaction that he had pulled out his clothes, then went to the bucket of water to wash his hands, recognized too late that it was disgustingly dirty, and was upset that now he could not wash his hands. Finally he pushed them into the sand. This option did not satisfy him, but he had to do what he could in the circumstances. Then he stood up and began to unbutton the coat of his uniform. As he did this, the two lady's handkerchiefs, which he had pushed into the back of his collar, fell into his hands. "Here you have your handkerchiefs," he said and threw them over to the Condemned Man. And to the Traveller he said by way of an explanation, "Presents from the ladies.

In spite of the obvious speed with which he took off the coat of his uniform and then undressed himself completely, he handled each piece of clothing very carefully, even running his fingers over the silver braids on his tunic with special care and shaking a tassel into place. But in great contrast to this care, as soon he was finished handling an article of clothing, he immediately flung it angrily into the hole. The last items he had left were his short sword and its harness. He pulled the sword out of its scabbard, broke it in pieces, gathered up everything—the pieces of the sword, the scabbard, and the harness—and threw them away so forcefully that they rattled against each other down in the pit.

Now he stood there naked. The Traveller bit his lip and said nothing. For he was aware what would happen, but he had no right to hinder the Officer in any way. If the judicial process to which the Officer clung was really so close to the point of being cancelled—perhaps as a result of the intervention of the Traveller, something to which he for his part felt duty-bound—then the Officer was now acting in a completely correct manner. In his place, the Traveller would not have acted any differently.

The Soldier and the Condemned Man at first did not understand a thing. To begin with they did not look, not even once. The Condemned Man was extremely happy to get the handkerchiefs back, but he could not enjoy them very long, for the Soldier snatched them from him with a quick grab, which he had not anticipated. The Condemned Man then tried to pull the handkerchiefs out from the Soldier's belt, where he had put them for safe keeping, but the Soldier was too wary. So they were fighting, half in jest. Only when the Officer was fully naked did they start to pay attention. The Condemned Man especially seemed to be struck by a premonition of some sort of significant transformation. What had happened to him was now taking place with the Officer. Perhaps this time the procedure would play itself out to its conclusion. The foreign Traveller had probably given the order. So that was revenge. Without having suffered all the way to the end himself, nonetheless he would be completely avenged. A wide, silent laugh now appeared on his face and did not go away.

The Officer, however, had turned towards the machine. If earlier on it had already become clear that he understood the machine thoroughly, one might well get alarmed now at the way he handled it and how it obeyed. He only had to bring his hand near the Harrow for it to rise and sink several times, until it had reached the correct position to make room for him. He only had to grasp the Bed by the edges, and it already began to quiver. The stump of felt moved up to his mouth. One could see how the Officer really did not want to accept it, but his hesitation was only momentary—he immediately submitted and took it in. Everything was ready, except that the straps still hung down on the sides. But they were clearly unnecessary.

The Officer did not have to be strapped down. When the Condemned Man saw the loose straps, he thought the execution would be incomplete unless they were fastened. He waved eagerly to the Soldier, and they ran over to strap in the Officer. The latter had already stuck out his foot to kick the crank designed to set the Inscriber in motion. Then he saw the two men coming. So he pulled his foot back and let himself be strapped in. But now he could no longer reach the crank. Neither the Soldier nor the Condemned Man would find it, and the Traveller was determined not to touch it. But that was unnecessary. Hardly were the straps attached when the machine already started working. The Bed quivered, the needles danced on his skin, and the Harrow swung up and down. The Traveller had already been staring for some time before he remembered that a wheel in the Inscriber was supposed to squeak. But everything was quiet, without the slightest audible hum.

Because of its silent working, the machine did not really attract attention. The Traveller looked over at the Soldier and the Condemned Man. The Condemned Man was the livelier of the two. Everything in the machine interested him. At times he bent down, at other times he stretched up, always pointing with his forefinger in order to show something to the Soldier. For the Traveller it was embarrassing. He was determined to remain here until the end, but he could no longer endure the sight of the two men. "Go home," he said. The Soldier might have been ready to do that, but the Condemned Man took the order as a direct punishment. With his hands folded he begged and pleaded to be allowed to stay there. And when the Traveller shook his head and was unwilling to give in, he even knelt down. Seeing that orders were of no help here, the Traveller wanted to go over and chase the two away.

Then he heard a noise from up in the Inscriber. He looked up. So was the gear wheel going out of alignment? But it was something else. The lid on the Inscriber was lifting up slowly. Then it fell completely open. The teeth of a cog wheel were exposed and lifted up. Soon the entire wheel appeared. It was as if some huge force was compressing the Inscriber, so that there was no longer sufficient room for this wheel. The wheel rolled all the way to the edge of the Inscriber, fell down, rolled upright a bit in the sand, and then fell over and lay still. But already up on the Inscriber another gear wheel was moving upwards. Several others followed—large ones, small ones, ones hard to distinguish. With each of them the same thing happened. One kept thinking that now the Inscriber must surely be empty, but then a new cluster with lots of parts would move up, fall down, roll in the sand, and lie still. With all this going on, the Condemned Man totally forgot the Traveller's order. The gear wheels completely delighted him. He kept wanting to grab one, and at the same time he was urging the Soldier to help him.

But he kept pulling his hand back startled, for immediately another wheel followed, which, at least in its initial rolling, surprised him.

The Traveller, by contrast, was very upset. Obviously the machine was breaking up. Its quiet operation had been an illusion. He felt as if he had to look after the Officer, now that the latter could no longer look after himself. But while the falling gear wheels were claiming all his attention, he had neglected to look at the rest of the machine. However, when he now bent over the Harrow, once the last gear wheel had left the Inscriber, he had a new, even more unpleasant surprise. The Harrow was not writing but only stabbing, and the Bed was not rolling the body, but lifting it, quivering, up into the needles. The Traveller wanted to reach in to stop the whole thing, if possible. This was not the torture the Officer wished to attain. It was murder, pure and simple. He stretched out his hands. But at that point the Harrow was already moving upwards and to the side, with the skewered body—just as it did in other cases, but only in the twelfth hour. Blood flowed out in hundreds of streams, not mixed with water—the water tubes had also failed to work this time. Then one last thing went wrong: the body would not come loose from the needles. Its blood streamed out, but it hung over the pit without falling. The Harrow wanted to move back to its original position, but, as if realizing that it could not free itself of its load, it remained over the hole.

"Help," the Traveller yelled out to the Soldier and the Condemned Man and grabbed the Officer's feet. He wanted to push against the feet himself and have the two others grab the Officer's head from the other side, so he could be slowly taken off the needles. But now the two men could not make up their mind whether to come or not. The Condemned Man turned away at once. The Traveller had to go over to him and drag him to the Officer's head by force. At this point, almost against his will, he looked at the face of the corpse. It was as it had been in his life. He could discover no sign of the promised transfiguration. What all the others had found in the machine, the Officer had not. His lips were pressed firmly together, his eyes were open and looked as they had when he was alive, his gaze was calm and convinced. The tip of a large iron needle had gone through his forehead.

* * *

As the Traveller, with the Soldier and the Condemned Man behind him, came to the first houses in the colony, the Soldier pointed to one and said, "That's the tea house."

On the ground floor of one of the houses was a deep, low room, like a cave, with smoke covered walls and ceiling. On the street side it was open along its full width.

Although there was little difference between the tea house and the rest of the houses in the colony, which were all very dilapidated, except for the Commandant's palatial structure, the Traveller was struck by the impression of historical memory, and he felt the power of earlier times. Followed by his companions, he walked closer, going between the unoccupied tables, which stood in the street in front of the tea house, and took a breath of the cool, stuffy air which came from inside. "The old man is buried here," said the Soldier; "a place in the cemetery was denied him by the chaplain. For a long time people were undecided where they should bury him. Finally they buried him here. Of course, the Officer explained none of that to you, for naturally he was the one most ashamed about it. A few times he even tried to dig up the old man at night, but he was always chased off." "Where is the grave?" asked the Traveller, who could not believe the Soldier. Instantly both men, the Soldier and the Condemned Man, ran in front of him and with hands outstretched pointed to the place where the grave was located. They led the Traveller to the back wall, where guests were sitting at a few tables. They were presumably dock workers, strong men with short, shiny, black beards. None of them wore coats, and their shirts were torn. They were poor, oppressed people. As the Traveller came closer, a few got up, leaned against the wall, and looked at him. A whisper went up around the Traveller—"It's a foreigner. He wants to look at the grave." They pushed one of the tables aside, under which there was a real grave stone. It was a simple stone, low enough for it to remain hidden under a table. It bore an inscription in very small letters. In order to read it the Traveller had to kneel down. It read, "Here rests the Old Commandant. His followers, who are now not permitted to have a name, buried him in this grave and erected this stone. There exists a prophecy that the Commandant will rise again after a certain number of years and from this house will lead his followers to a re conquest of the colony. Have faith and wait!"

When the Traveller had read it and got up, he saw the men standing around him and smiling, as if they had read the inscription with him, found it ridiculous, and were asking him to share their opinion. The Traveller acted as if he had not noticed, distributed some coins among them, waited until the table was pushed back over the grave, left the tea house, and went to the harbour.

In the tea house the Soldier and the Condemned Man had come across some people they knew who detained them. However, they must have broken free of them soon, because by the time the Traveller found himself in the middle of a long staircase which led to the boats, they were already running after him. They probably wanted to force the Traveller at the last minute to take them with him.

While the Traveller was haggling at the bottom of the stairs with a sailor about his passage out to the steamer, the two men were racing down the steps in silence, for they did not dare cry out. But as they reached the bottom, the Traveller was already in the boat, and the sailor at once cast off from shore. They could still have jumped into the boat, but the Traveller picked up a heavy knotted rope from the boat bottom, threatened them with it, and thus prevented them from jumping in.

Story 16

JOSEPHINE THE SONGSTRESS

Josephine is the name of our songstress. Those who have never heard her sing simply haven't experienced the power of song. Everyone who hears her is pulled out of him or herself, transported, and this is yet more of a mystery since our race as a whole has no great love for music. Peace and quiet (Stiller Frieden) are what we yearn for more than anything our lives are hard such is the music that, generally, we love above all others, we just don't have it in us after another long day of work in which we strive to do our best in dispensing with a thousand and one cares, there's just nothing left over with which we might pull ourselves to the distant heights, so far removed, where music comes alive. But we don't generally shed any tears over this, not once do we go so far as to lament our loss, it's just at least this is my personal opinion on the subject it's just a minor irrelevancy. There's a certain sort of sly cleverness that kicks in here, one, indeed, that we need terribly: we consider this as being our greatest asset and we use it to laugh off any and all criticism and to console ourselves about everything. Such is our way, such cleverness in all things practical; indeed, it kicks in even should there be some yearning though there isn't but if there were to be such a yearning for the sublime happiness (Glück) that music may, perhaps, deliver. Only Josephine makes an exception, she loves music and knows how to deliver its power, and she's the only one, when she's gone then music too will disappear, and who knows for how long, right out of the midst of our lives. I've thought about this quite often, essentially what is it about music, how does it come alive and touch us so deeply. After all, we're not particularly inclined toward music, indeed, we tend to be rather adverse, so how can it be that we have any understanding of Josephine's performances?... or, since she contends that we don't understand, why is it that we believe that we do? The simplest answer is quite simply that the beauty of her singing is so powerful that even the greatest antagonism is outdone, such sensibilities crumble in her presence but this answer is hardly satisfactory, not at all. For if it really were to be true then one would always have to have a feeling for the other worldliness, that something was sounding forth from out of her throat that we have never heard before, something that we don't, truth to tell, even have a capacity for hearing, that we become capable of hearing it only when Josephine sings, she and she alone, nobody else delivers. But from my vantage I'd have to say that this just isn't so, at least I haven't had such an experience and I haven't been able to observe anyone else experiencing something like this either.

In private conversations amongst trusted friends we admit this quite openly, that Josephine's songs aren't, as songs go, anything all that out of the ordinary, there's nothing essentially miraculous about them. And, is it even song at all? Despite our fundamental lack in things musical we do have a substantial history that has come down to us about singing; in earlier times our forefathers were musical there are legends that inform us about all of this and, indeed, even still we have some of these songs though, to be sure, nobody has any idea as to how they're to be sung. I don't know why it is that in the course of centuries we became so thoroughly disinterested in any sort of music, that, indeed, we became fundamentally hostile toward it, perhaps this is due to our particular destiny, that somehow we were chosen for this: that we worship stillness, stepping back within ourselves and not really being committed and, so, in all actuality we don't have much choice in this. But however all of this may be, we still do have some premonition of what song is and our premonition, to be perfectly honest, goes against her artistry, what Josephine actually does when she's singing. For, taken in an absolute sense, is this really singing at all? perhaps, indeed, all that she really manages to do is a sort of whistling? And everybody knows whistling inside and out, this is the core artistry of our folk or, rather, it's not even deserving of the name "art," rather it's simply how you would characterize us, this is what we do: a soft kind of whistling with an undercurrent that hisses; and there's really just two sorts: the melancholic, ascetic, dreamy sort that typically is weak and pervasive; and then there's the triumphant, full bodied tone that tends to have sharp contours. Thus, we're all natural born whistlers and nobody would ever think about labeling this as being art; sure, now and again somebody might do a bit of research into this propensity of ours and how it contributes to some particular topic, but in general everybody whistles without even thinking about it and, indeed, without even so much as noticing it and, moreover, it's quite certain that the greater majority don't even know that whistling is the one characteristic that defines who we are most intimately.

If, then, if it were to be true that Josephine doesn't sing but just whistles, and indeed, as it seems to me, that her whistling barely exceeds the bounds of the ordinary, that really her powers in whistling don't even extend into the triumphant sort mentioned earlier whereas the whistling of our typical laborer, someone who is quite down to earth and who whistles the whole day long without any particular effort, that this just goes hand in hand with his earthly travails, well, if all of this were to be true then, indeed, Josephine's purported artistry would be refuted but now, first and foremost, now we'd have to face up to this riddle as to why it is that her performances are so electrifying! And really, when you get right down to it, it's not merely whistling, this is not everything that Josephine exhibits in her performances you need only place yourself in the back of the auditorium and listen attentively... or, better yet, test this out in the following manner: if Josephine is singing amongst a group of others and if you should give yourself the task of making her voice out from amongst these others then without fail you won't be able to distinguish anything else but a typical, middle-of-the-road sort of whistling that, at the most, is a bit sweeter or somehow softer and this is the only distinguishing characteristic that you might hear. But then, if you stand there in front of her so it's not merely whistling, there's yet another component that's absolutely required if one is to understand her art properly, namely that you don't merely listen to her, rather you also have to see her. Even if it were to be nothing more than our everyday whistling, still there's this oddity of how she presents herself, the drama and theatrics of her performance that someone would put on such airs and then do nothing more than what's typical, the ordinary, middle-of-the-road sort of whistling. Cracking pecans doesn't entail any particular artistry, none whatsoever, hence nobody would be so daring as to gather up an audience and then for his performance that he would shell a pound of pecans. But, all the same, if one were to do just this and if one's performance were to be a great success, well then, obviously it couldn't possibly simply be a matter of cracking nuts! Or maybe it does have something to do with nut-cracking but it suddenly has become apparent that there's more to cracking nuts than meets the eye, that we've been overlooking something because we just happen to be so good at it and that only now its innermost essence has been put up on display whereby it is even quite conceivable that this might be a distinct advantage and quite useful, namely that the artist performing such a feat isn't really all that good at cracking nuts to begin with. Perhaps just this is the proper correlation for our appreciation of Josephine's musical performances: that we stand in awe before her for doing something that we do all the time ourselves without being amazed in the least. In any event, we're all on her side, we find ourselves totally 'at one' with her and we agree about this. Once I was present as somebody as only might be expected somebody was pointing out to her how our folk in general tend to whistle, and he was quite modest and matter of fact in how he brought this up, like if someone would have been talking to somebody who is rich and might mention by the way that although he isn't rich himself, all the same, he isn't starving, and that by mentioning this one isn't trying to hurt this well heeled lolloper at all, that rather he should go ahead and enjoy his wealth without any worries about it.

But for Josephine this was just too much! she got so cheeky, such a superior, condescending smile played upon her lips such as, until then, I had never seen she whose external demeanor is truly as sweet as sweet can be, that even in our folk where the fair sex always tend toward being affable, Josephine still stands out in her charming amiability... but now she seemed downright crude; it may be that due to her heightened sensibilities as an "artiste" she noticed this right away too and, so, she got a better grip upon herself. In any event, she denied that there might be any relation whatsoever between her art and whistling and for those who think otherwise all that she has is contempt and, most probably, pure hatred that, naturally, she tries to cover up and she won't even admit it to herself. And it's not as if she did this for her own benefit since these contrarians to which camp I myself halfway belong we don't find her performances to be any less amazing than everybody else, we're just as much amongst the overwhelming crowd of her admirers; but Josephine, Josephine doesn't want simply that she amaze her audience, rather she wants to amaze us in her own particular manner, amazement in itself doesn't mean a thing to her. And when you take your seat in her auditorium then you understand her position, opposition is only possible at a great distance; sitting there before her it's quite clear that what she's whistling is no whistling. Since whistling belongs amongst our unconscious habits, our second nature as it were, so you might think that people would whistle in her auditorium; after all we feel good in her presence and we tend to whistle whenever we're feeling good; but nobody whistles in her presence, rather, it's as still as still can be quiet as a mouse it's as if the peace that we yearn for and which our whistling would disturb, it's as if this peace were to be partially granted to us and, so, we stay silent. Is it her singing that so captivates us?... or rather, much more, is it the celebratory sobriety of our stillness that encompasses her weak, little voice? It once happened that some small urchin, an innocent little thing, started into whistling during one of Josephine's performances. Now, it was quite the same as what we were hearing from Josephine there up in front and totally unconcerned about this unexpected variation in her routine Josephine continued right on in her timid whistling, and so here within the public this little chickabiddy having inadvertently forgotten herself was whistling along too...

But you better believe we hissed and whistled this disturbing non entity back to silence and did so even despite the fact that this wouldn't really have been necessary for it's quite certain that the little thing would have been happiest if she could have crept away on all fours and hidden herself in some hole due to her shame and angst whilst in the meantime Josephine's vocal prowess started into whistling triumphantly and due to herself satisfaction she became practically ecstatic, what with her arms splayed out to her sides and her throat that couldn't possibly be extended any further. In any event, all of this is simply standard fare for Josephine any minor irrelevancy, some chance event, the most picayune disorder or bit of unruliness, a creaking noise coming from somewhere high up in the parquet, somebody who's gritting their teeth, even the slightest malfunction in the lighting, she uses all of these to heighten the effect of her performance, in her opinion she's singing to deaf ears anyway though there's never any deficiency in spirited enthusiasm or applause but then, in respect to any real understanding in the particular way that Josephine means it, well, this is just something that she's learned to do without and so all of these disturbances simply play into her hand, everything that conspires against the absolute purity of her voice, all of this is an easy battle, indeed it's no battle at all, simply by means of this contrast she comes off victorious, all of this helps her along to wake up the crowd, not that this would teach them any real understanding but still it teaches respect, it gives them a premonition of what's at stake. And it wouldn't be beyond the pale that one might think that she just for instance that she herself had somehow had a hand in instigating that the little take formerly mentioned might pipe up if only this wasn't contradicted by her dream like, confused state that hasn't the least bit of concern nor any respect for doing anything in accordance to the normal strictures of cause and effect, rather she's always acting 'the artiste.' And if small co incidences play into her hand how much more so would the great. Our life is so terribly beset by strife, every day brings its share of rude surprises, fears, hopes and shocking outrages it's simply impossible that any one of us might bear it, fortunately the individual gains strength by being carried along day and night upon the shoulders of the community, but even so it's terribly bleak and difficult, often enough millions of our folk tremble beneath the weight of the burden that is placed upon just one. Then Josephine intuits that her time has come. Already she's standing there, the tender soul, there's a spot beneath her breast that in rapport to the angst of the times starts to vibrate, it's as if all of her powers were gathered up within her piteous song, as if everything that wasn't directly involved in her expressing her song, all extraneous concerns, powers and possibilities were removed, that she's totally stripped, sacrificed and under the mercy and protection of angelic beings, as if she were so exposed that during this interval of her rapture whilst her inner being is so taken up in expressing song, well, a cold draft of air that simply might be passing by would be all that it would take to kill her.

But it's precisely in such moments as these with this spectacle before us, it's then that we contrarians and we're the first to admit our contrariness it's now that we can't help but to remark to one another: She can't even manage to whistle decently, just look at how she finds herself into knots and not that she'd be singing let's not talk about song but just so that she might force out a smidgen of piping, the regular sort of whistling that's heard even in the most rustic parts of our homeland. So it seems to us, but, as I already mentioned, this is simply a momentary impression and one that is a necessary preamble but also one that passes very quickly. Already we're being enveloped by the receptive feelings of the multitude, the warmth of the crowd with one body pressed up upon the next, all so timid and listening in rapt attention and with bated breath. And that a crowd gather, us we whose lives are always being thrown about this way and that, always in a great rush to get somewhere, though not that we'd have any clear conception as to what all the ruckus really means and all that Josephine generally needs to do is throw back her head, open up her little mouth halfway, her eyes resting upon some visage up in the heights and, so, she assumes her stance that announces to us that now she's ready to sing. She can do this wherever she likes, it doesn't have to be in a spot that's particularly accessible, any hide-away will do, some corner that she's picked out just as her mood strikes her, some spur of the moment decision, any spot is as good as the next. The news that she's ready to sing travels fast and in no time the procession of listeners is streaming in. Now from time to time, indeed, there are hindrances that crop up; it's during times of calamity that Josephine loves to sing most of all and it's even then that our cares and urgent concerns become as wide ranging as they can be and they drive us into paths that are utterly diverse; even with the best of wills it's not always possible to assemble a crowd on a moment's notice in accordance to Josephine's mood and, so, she's left standing there in her great pose for a longer period without having a sufficient audience... then, indeed, then she becomes enraged, livid she'll start stamping her feet and cursing, the things that she says! Unladylike in the extreme, indeed, she even bites. But, all the same, even this doesn't wreck havoc on her reputation, rather than try to talk sense into her everyone does their utmost to fulfill her expectations, messengers are dispatched to expedite the gathering of an audience; but this isn't done openly, it's all kept hush-hush, one notices that sentries have been posted at various intersections and these clever accomplices have a special way of winking at you that you'd better get moving a bit quicker and all of this happens behind the scenes until finally a sufficient crowd has come together.

Now, what is it that spurs our folk on, that we make every effort in satisfying Josephine's whims? This question isn't any easier to answer than the underlying question to which it's easily tied, to wit: What is it about Josephine's songs, why is it that we're so captivated by them? The first question could be struck out all together as being totally subordinate to the second, if only we were able to affirm that our folk really is committed to Josephine be it because of her songs or due to whatever else in an unqualified way. But then, this isn't the case either, there's hardly anything to which our folk is committed in an unqualified manner, we hardly know what we're to think of such limitless adoration; our folk, these critters that, indeed, love that sort of cleverness which, in itself, is quite harmless: childish whisperings, the chitter-chatter that proves how well we're able to bring our lips into motion, how far is it from us that we'd ever say anything bad, such a folk is simply incapable of devoting itself to anything without some qualification... and Josephine has a feeling for all of this, she's nobody's fool and, indeed, it's even precisely this that she's up against, fighting against it with all of the strength she can muster with her weak throat. But now, naturally, one also mustn't go too far in such general platitudes, one always has to reserve one's judgment and, verily, our folk is devoted to Josephine, just not unconditionally. For instance, nobody would ever find it allowable to laugh at Josephine. One is permitted to admit this much: there's an awful lot about Josephine that tends toward the comic, in and of itself we all enjoy having a good laugh, despite all of the misery and absurdity of our lives we're always ready, at least to a certain extent, to crack a good joke about whatever it ever may be, but we don't ever crack jokes on Josephine's account. Sometimes I get the impression that our folk conceives its relationship to Josephine in the following manner: that she, this fragile, attention dependent, extraordinary (and in her own opinion extraordinary due to her singing) this entity, Josephine, would be entrusted to us and that it would be incumbent upon us that we take good care of her; whatever underlies all of this probably isn't particularly clear to anybody but still this fact remains apparent nonetheless. One simply doesn't make jokes about someone over whom you are entrusted; you can laugh about yourself but not about your fledgling, laughing about such a being would be tantamount to breaking your pledge, a dereliction of duty; it is the extreme in maliciousness when those amongst us having malice inflict upon Josephine the following observation, an observation that I've heard from time to time: that when Josephine comes before us we lose our capacity to laugh. Thus it is that our folk cares for Josephine in the manner of a father who has taken on the burden of bringing up a child, a child whose arms are stretched out toward you, one doesn't know whether these hands are pleading or exacting.

The overriding concern is unavoidable: do we have it in us that we tend our foster child as is required? But, in all actuality, in this particular instance we fulfill our responsibilities impeccably. I certainly could never do it alone, nor could anybody else do so as an individual, but what nobody is capable of doing alone we do manage and most readily manage to accomplish as a community. To be sure, the difference in power between the folk as a whole and their fledgling is so immense, it's already quite sufficient when we pull the tender thing within the warmth bestowed by our community, already this alone suffices and our fledgling is protected. Admittedly, nobody would dare to discuss such things with Josephine. "Phooey on your protection" she'd pipe up. "Yea, yea: whistle as you will" that's what we'd think, but we'd never say it. And beyond all of this it's not truly a refutation when she acts so rebelliously, much rather this is simply what's natural and what one should expect from a child, this is the way that children demonstrate their thanks and, then too, it's in the nature of a father that he simply ignores the whole thing and goes his merry way. Now, there's a lot more in play here that's quite difficult to explain simply in hindsight to the relation sketched above, this relation between our folk and Josephine. Namely, Josephine is wont to take a position that is diametrically the opposite to this, she believes that it falls upon her and her alone, that she protects us, the community. The way that she sees it is that it's only through her songs that we are to be saved from all of the evil inherent in our political and economic reality, it's nothing short of this that under lies her singing, and even if it should be true that these songs are incapable of driving away and dispelling all of our misfortune and misery (Unglück), the sad lot of our destiny, well at least they will give us the strength so that we might bear them. Indeed, she doesn't say it quite like this, nor would she say anything else but this, point of fact, she hardly talks at all, she remains silent amongst the blathering bimbos; but still, this is the fire that blazes from out of her eyes, this is what lurks behind her tight lipped glare; but amongst us there's hardly a soul who can hold his mouth shut and refrain from chattering, but she can do this, it's writ large on her features. By every piece of bad news, and on most days the bad news far outweighs the good, any number of horrible reports flow in upon us and each one of them overrunning the previous, and all of them borne along amongst an awesome amount of lies and half truths, when suddenly she gets the urge to rise up to the occasion though on most days all of this just weighs her down closer to the floorboards but now she's pulled herself up and is extending her throat out, she's trying to get an encompassing view over her flock just as if she were a shepherdess overseeing her sheep before an approaching storm.

Certainly, there are also children who rebel against the ways of the world in such a wild, uncontrolled manner, but with

Josephine this has a foundation that has a bit more substance. Though, indeed, she doesn't save us, nor does she supply us with any powers that might be decisive, it's all too easy to play the role of savior when you're dealing with such a folk like us: we're used to suffering, well acquainted with death, not given to pretense, fast in our decision making, only apparently angst ridden in this atmosphere of great daring and heroics in which we're constantly making do, living out our lives and, beyond all of this, our fertility is as legend as our audaciousness; it is so easy as I've said that one plays oneself off as the savior for such a folk, a folk that somehow or other manages to save itself though not, let us never forget, not without terrible sacrifices over which the historians, and in general we really do neglect doing all that much in viable historical research, the historians, as I say, those who preserve the actual in their memories of the past: their blood runs cold and simply paralyzes them due to the shocking horror, all of the horrors through which we've come! But still it is true that in the times of our greatest despair, this is when we listen most attentively to Josephine's voice. All of the forebodings, the threats that are gathering above us, all of this tends to make us calmer and more humble, we're more easily molded and responsive to Josephine's commanding presence, we're more than happy to gather together and press up against one another and even the more so due to the circumstance that our gathering is far removed from the major dilemma that torments us. It's as if we'd want a quick true, all too true, speed is always paramount, this is something that Josephine is wont to forget all too readily a quick pick me up, to drink a cup from the fountain of peace before venturing out into the calamities of battle. It's not so much a vocal performance as it is an assemblage of the populace, an assemblage in which except for the slight whistling coming from center stage up front, besides this it's totally silent, the hour is far too serious for any idle gossip!

Such a relation is not what is needed and it's impossible that this, indeed, would ever satisfy Josephine, nor is this even something that might be maintained for long. Despite all of her nervous anguish that overcomes her, filling her with unhappiness due to her position that has never been clarified, there's a great deal that she, blinded by her self-consciousness, doesn't see, and it doesn't take all that much effort for her blind spot to be enlarged considerably, there's a swarm of her adherents who are constantly flattering her, egging her on, and in doing this they perform a useful function though, to be sure, all of this happens off to one side and out of the limelight, that she might sing for them in some remote corner, and were it not for them it's certain that she'd never have the nerve to pull off the sacrifice needed to sing, that she do so even despite the enormity of the undertaking.

And it's not as if it were all for nothing for then her artistic performance doesn't remain unnoticed. Despite the fact that we're consumed with matters that are wholly 'other' and that our stillness is not simply due to our devoted appreciation of hearing her sing, that there are quite a few of us who don't even cast our eyes her way, rather there are so many whose faces are pressed into the fur of their neighbor, and so it seems as if Josephine's performance was all for nothing, that her great effort would be futile, all the same one cannot deny it, something does force its way through, something of her whistling inevitably does strike us. Such a whistling that rises up where everyone else is required to remain silent, this just about comes off as a messenger of the folk to the individual, Josephine's diaphanous whistling right into the midst of the dead seriousness of the decisive decisions, this is almost a metaphor for the impoverished nature of our folk's existence in the midst of the tumult of a hostile world, a world that, quite simply, is over brimming with enemies. Josephine makes her stand, this excuse of a voice, this nothingness, this abysmal execution asserts itself and creates a path to us it does one good to reflect upon this; were we to have a real artist, someone who actually could sing, if ever such a one might appear amongst us it's quite certain that we wouldn't be able to bear it in times like these and with one voice we'd denounce the senselessness of such a performance. May Josephine be protected from ever recognizing this fact, the fact that simply by listening to her, this itself proves that her artistic performance isn't really song. Most probably she has some premonition of this why else would it be that she's so insistent in denying that we'd be listening to her; but she always sings anyway, she whistles her tunes in spite of her premonition. But, all the same, there is yet a consolation for her for, indeed, to a certain extent we really do listen, probably in a similar manner as one would listen to a genuine artist, she achieves results that such an artist would be vain to attempt in our presence and that are only to be achieved quite specifically by means that are insufficient. This, very probably, this is connected to the way that our lives are structured. In our folk nobody has any experience of youth, there's barely even any time for being a toddler.

Now and again efforts are made in this direction, one should really let the children be children, they need their own special freedom, their own considerations, a protected space, they have a right to a carefree existence, a bit of romping about, some rolling and tumbling, a little playtime everybody likes to agree with this, we all do what we can to bring this about, it's a grand promotion and there's practically nobody who says anything to the contrary, there's basically nothing that is worth promoting if this isn't but, then too, there's also nothing that's so impossible to realize, such contradicts the reality of our lives; one agrees wholeheartedly with the promotion, one attempts to do what one can to fulfill the good sense that is inherent in it but before you know it everything has reverted back to the way it was before. Our life is as it is;

a child, just as soon as he's learned to move about a little and as soon as he can differentiate amongst his surroundings, so he has to take care of himself just like an adult; all of the areas in which due to the economic realities that govern our lives we are forced to live our lives all scattered about, well, such a space is too big, our enemies are way too numerous, all of the dangers are beyond our powers of calculation... there's just no way that we could keep our children apart, secluded from the fight for survival, if we even were to attempt to do so this itself would mean their premature end. Beyond all of this, so sad as all of the previous is, there's yet another factor, something a bit more uplifting, the fertility of our tribe. Each generation and every one of them is bounteous each presses upon the next and drives them forth; the children simply don't have any time in which they might be children. It may well be so that with other folk the children are carefully tended, that schools are built for them, that the little darlings stream into these schools on a daily basis, that they are heralded as the future of the race, looking up beauteously toward the visage (Anblick) of the patriot, so in such circumstances it's always the same children attending school for a longer period of time, going to school and coming back from school. We don't have any schools but in practically no time at all there come hoards and hoards of our children, you can't see any end to them, they come hissing or peeping for so long as they haven't learned how to whistle, they come propelled forward, waltzing along or rolling forth until they've learned how to run properly, clumsily they feel their way about through thick and thin until they've trained their eyes to see things properly our children! And it's not as it was with the formerly mentioned schools, over and over the same children in attendance, no it's always new ones, never ending, not even pausing, barely has a new child appeared and it's no longer a child, there are already new faces that are forcing their way through from behind, an undifferentiated mass in their teeming multitude and their hurry, pink in their blessed happiness (Glück). Indeed, no matter how beauteous all of this may be and despite how envious others may be, and rightfully so, all the same there's simply no way that we would be able to provide our children with a viable childhood, one that is real. Naturally, there are consequences.

There's a certain ever present, not to be liquidated childishness that permeates our folk; this exists in stark contradiction to that which we hold as being our best trait: our practical matter-of-factness and considerable know how which rises above all deceit. We often act in ways that are totally and utterly ridiculous and, indeed, precisely like children we do things that are crazy, letting loose with our assets in a manner that is bereft of all rationality, prodigious in our celebrations, partaking in a light headed frivolousness that is divorced from all sensibility, and often enough all simply for the sake of some small token of fun, so much do we love having our small amusements. And even though, naturally, the extent of our power of having such childish joys is no longer as fulfilling as is the case with children, all the same it is certain that there's yet a bit of this that remains. Isn't it, perhaps, isn't it just this childishness of our folk from which Josephine, too, is profiting? But our folk isn't only childish, to a certain extent we also age prematurely, childhood and old age mix themselves differently with us than by others. We don't have any youth, we jump right away into maturity and, then, we remain grown-ups for too long and as a consequence to this there's a broad shadow of a certain tiredness and a sort of hopelessness that colours our essential nature, a nature that as a whole is otherwise so tenacious and permeated by hope, strong hope. This, no doubt, this is related to why we're so disinclined toward music we're too old for music, so much excitement, so much passion doesn't sit well with our heaviness; with a wink our tired constitutions part ways from the music lovers, we've pulled ourselves back and find our contentment in whistling a bit of whistling now and then, this is what is right for us. And who knows as to whether, even yet, whether there might still be some talent for music that lurks within us... if there should be such the character of our folk would have to suppress it, we would never allow its development within our midst. On the other hand Josephine can go ahead and do what she pleases, whether it's whistling or if it should be singing or whatever she might want to name it call it what you will, this doesn't disturb us, rather this is just what we need, we're quite able to carry this along if there should be something of music within all of this, well, it has been reduced to a certain minimum, there have been allowances made for keeping up with a certain amount of our musical tradition, just as long as this doesn't have any real impact upon us, nothing that might be a burden and weigh us down. But Josephine brings to us, a folk that is tuned in this manner, something more.

At her concerts, and most especially during troubled times, there's only a small few who take any interest in the songstress herself, such as she is perhaps there's a fairly large group up there in the front rows who are curious as regards to how she manages to pucker her lips, how she forces the air out from between her dainty little teeth, that they experience a bit of awe and marvel over how the tone fades away and how she is able to use this transient dissolution to her own advantage, how she practically dies, putting herself out and thereby firing herself up for her subsequent performance, her song that becomes ever the less understandable as it progresses, but the essential mass of the populace this is very clear to see the multitude have retreated into themselves. Here in the meager pauses between its battles the folk finds itself in a dream state, it's as if the limbs of the individual were finally relaxed, as if those who are bereft of peace and calm were finally allowed to throw themselves upon the great bed of warmth of the folk where, then, they might stretch themselves. And within these dreams Josephine's whistling rings out here and there she calls this pearling, we call it stuttering but in any event it belongs here more than anywhere else, this is its place where it might be received as, then, music hardly ever finds any particular attentiveness bestowed upon it, there's just nobody out there waiting for the next great song. There's something of the poverty of our shortened childhood in this, something of what has been lost and of the bliss that we'll never be able to find again, but there's also something of our active day-to-day existence, something of the small, inconceivable gaiety that is yet there and which refuses to die and all of this, truly, all of this is not to be spoken using the great tones of brass instruments, rather it requires a light touch, a whisper, an intimate trust that sometimes talks a bit hoarsely. Naturally, it's a whistling how else? Whistling is the language in which we speak, though there's many a soul who whistles away for the entirety of his or her long life and doesn't even once know it, but here whistling has become freed from the chains of our daily lives, the restrictions that life forces upon us and, so, this frees us too if only for a little while. This is why we never wanted to miss these performances.

Should it perhaps be that in this manner Josephine was right after all when she made her claim that she infuses new powers into us during troubled times? How else could one explain it? Josephine's contingent of flatterers piped up in their uncritical impertinence how else was one to explain the great rush of the public, and especially under such dire circumstances that threatened us, a rush that, indeed, sometimes would prevent us from being able to mount a sufficient defence, that we do so in a timely manner! Now, the latter point is quite right but certainly this doesn't belong amongst Josephine's claims to fame, and most particularly not when one adds on that when her concerts were unexpectedly disrupted by an assault from our enemies and, indeed, there would be any number of casualties on our side, that many of us had to lay down our lives for the defence and Josephine, then, she who was totally responsible and who bore the guilt, indeed it might even have been her whistling itself that attracted our enemy's attention and drew him our way, Josephine was always in the safest spot and she was also the first to disappear, whisked away hurriedly and quietly amongst her protecting contingent of admirers. But this too, everybody knows that this, fundamentally, is just the way it is and all the same this doesn't slow anyone down the next time around, whenever and wherever Josephine may get carried away and express her devotion to music, taking it into her head to rise up and give us another of her performances. From this for this, indeed, is something that is extreme from this one could make the deduction that Josephine's position is one that basically stands outside of the law, that she is permitted to do whatever she pleases and that everything will be forgiven. If this really were to be the case then Josephine's contentions would be totally understandable yes, one could to a certain extent see in this freedom that the folk would have bestowed upon her, in such an extraordinary, uniquely privileged gift, this bestowal that truth to tell contradicts what the law requires, one could see a confirmation of the fact that, just as Josephine asserts, the folk doesn't understand anything at all of what she's about, that it stands helplessly in awe before her artistry, that it is unworthy and abashed by its incapacity and that as recompense for this 'wrong' that it has inflicted upon her, that all of these misunderstandings might be balanced out or at least it strives to balance them out that just as her art extends beyond their capacities of conceptualization, so too her person and her wishes are placed beyond their authority: that, in short, she is immune from the commands and from the powers of the ruling authority. Now, indeed, this isn't right utterly and totally not; perhaps as individuals our folk is liable to capitulate to Josephine's whims all too quickly but just as our folk doesn't capitulate to anyone at all in an unconditional manner, so too it doesn't do so for her. And it's quite easy to prove this. Already for quite some time, perhaps even right off from the beginning of herself promotion as an artiste, Josephine has fought for the privilege of being excused from doing any other work other than her singing that she should be released from all of the cares regarding the earning of one's daily bread and, likewise, from everything else that is somehow related to our struggle for survival, and that all of this should be placed, most probably, upon the shoulders of the entire community, upon our folk as a whole. There are idealists, people who are quick to grasp at the spirit I do believe that even yet there are a few such amongst us who simply due to the bold extravagance and oddity of such an assertion, that this spirited boldness all alone would be enough to convince them of the inner justification of such a stance. Well, our folk draws its own conclusions and doesn't waste a whole lot of time in calmly speaking its mind: No way José.

It also doesn't spend much time or effort in attempting to refute the principles upon which her contention is grounded. For instance, Josephine might point out that all of the efforts required in her taking care of her subsistence needs, all of this work simply detracts from her being able to train her voice, that her efforts, indeed, in doing this other work are relatively minor if you compare it to the efforts that are required for her singing, but that, all the same, this robs her of the possibility of recovering in an appropriate manner after all of the exertions that her singing requires and, then too, that she needs to strengthen herself so that she might reach ever new heights in her performances; in short that she's stretched herself right to the edge of her capacities and that under such circumstances she will never be able to attain the heights that, otherwise, she would be able to attain. The folk give her a hearing, it all goes in one ear and right out the other. This folk of ours, an entity that often enough is so easily swayed, sometimes we aren't to be budged at all, not even the smallest bit. Our refusal is sometimes so harsh and abrasive that Josephine herself is staggered by it... she seems to be coming to terms with it, she continues along doing her work just like everybody else, and she also continues right along with her singing doing as well as she's able, but just for a little while, then she renews her struggle with new found powers and for this there appears to be a reserve that's infinite. Now, it's really all too clear, Josephine isn't really and truly striving after that, what she has said literally in her words. She is, after all, a rational being, and she's not a bit shy about doing her fair share of the work just as none of us is adverse to working, our folk has always been known as being exceptionally industrious. Indeed, she'd go on doing her work and living her life as normal even if we were to give in to her request, her work doesn't really interfere with her singing and her singing wouldn't be improved, not one whit, it wouldn't become any more beauteous... no, what she's up to now is just another sort of publicity stunt, she's looking for something that demonstrates her uniqueness, something that will persevere throughout the ages, something that would lift her out from 'the normal' in recognition of her artistic achievement. Whereas she seems to be capable of achieving most everything else, this stubbornly resists, there's no giving in here, there's not even any wiggle room, none at all. Perhaps she shouldn't have ventured down this road in the first place, perhaps she's finally become aware that this was a big mistake right from the get go but now there's just no way back, reversing course would carry a stigma and be called: being untrue to oneself, now she has to stand or fall with this, her fate has become enmeshed with her petition.

If she had any real enemies as she says then they could simply stand back and observe the battle without even having to lift a finger, then it would just be an amusement. But she doesn't have a single enemy and even if it is true that there may be a few of us contrarians who object to this or that, that we do have a few minor criticisms, all the same there's certainly no one who enjoys entering into this particular fray with her. Indeed, we steer clear of the whole topic since in respect to this our position is simply as firm as ice, nobody wants to be a judge in such a frigid matter, we're hardly ever to be found putting ourselves into such a position. And even if as regards this matter such a cold judgment is all that can be expected, nonetheless the very idea that our folk would relate to itself in such a cold manner, this precludes the possibility of anyone finding any joy in stating what's obvious. What we're dealing with here and no matter from which side you might look at it, whether from Josephine's petition or if it should be from our side of denial in either case it's not really the matter itself that's at issue but, more so, the basic idea that our folk might cut itself apart from itself and throw up such an impenetrable wall and, indeed, all the more impenetrable when you consider that Josephine is one of us, that we relate to her as a father and, indeed, as more than a father, as someone who is humbly taking care of its tender fledgling. Now, if there were to be one individual rather than the whole of our folk placed in such a position one might very well come to the belief that such a father figure would simply start giving in to all of Josephine's demands so that finally, after having allowed her far more than ever would be justified, finally a limit would have to appear all on its own, that by always saying "yes" to her unreasonable requests, by always allowing her more and more rope with which she might hang herself, well, sooner or later she'd reach the far end of her tether and the matter would become as clear as day; in short: that by giving in such an exorbitant manner the final refusal would be sped up and it would then resound with a short, crisp finality that couldn't be mistaken. Now, certainly, this isn't an accurate portrayal of how this relation is structured, our folk hasn't any need of such clever tactics and, beyond this, our respect for Josephine is long standing and couldn't be any more earnest and, moreover, Josephine's request is so blatantly black and white that any child you might ask wouldn't have the least bit of hesitation in telling you what the outcome would be; but in spite of all of this it may well be that Josephine already has a grasp of this matter, that she has a clear premonition of all of this and that this simply plays into it, leaving a bitter aftertaste on top of the indignity of our refusal. But, be this as it may, whether she has such a premonition or not, this doesn't instill any fear into her or keep her from plunging into this battle.

Indeed, as of late she's even intensified her attack... whereas before she was content to pursue her objective merely through verbal means, just through words, now she's starting to expand her repertoire, extending her fight into domains that she believes may be more efficacious, but it's our opinion that her new tactics are more likely to backfire right back in her face and prove to be more dangerous for herself. There are many of us who believe that Josephine is becoming so adamant about this whole escapade because she's beginning to feel old, that she hasn't all that much time left before her voice will start to weaken and, thus, it's high time that she enter into this last decisive battle for achieving the recognition that's due. But I don't believe it. Josephine wouldn't be Josephine if this were to be true. For her there's no such thing as "getting old," and her voice will never weaken. If she's demanding something so what's behind it all are inner principles, she'd never allow herself to be swayed by any external considerations. She's grasping for the highest wreath not because it so happens that it's momentarily hanging a bit lower, rather simply because it is the ultimate if it should lie within her powers she'd hang it higher yet. Such a noble regard for the spiritual doesn't, however, keep her from stooping down and using means that are most base. Her right to do just as she pleases, this is something about which she's never had any doubts. What difference does it make which means she uses just as long as she's able to obtain her objective and, indeed, particularly when you consider that the way she judges the world there's simply no way to get 'there' if she were to restrict herself to doing things in the ways that are respected. Perhaps it's even for this reason that she's switched in her tactics and no longer pursues her goal merely from the realm of song, that rather she's shifted to an arena that is less dear. Her circle of admirers has been letting it be known that Josephine has a definite feeling that she's able to sing in such a manner that the entirety of our folk in all of its divisions, and even right into the most entrenched opposition, everyone would find real pleasure in hearing her and she's not meaning real pleasure in the typical sense of our folk, our folk has always asserted to have found pleasure in listening to Josephine, rather she's meaning pleasure in a sense all her own, pleasure in the sense of her striving. But, she's quick to add on: since there's just no way that she might ever prove to be false to that which is highest, nor could she possibly stoop to a level that would flatter the commoners, well, matters are simply going to have to remain just as they are.

But then, in respect to her battle of becoming free from doing any work, here things are different; indeed, this too is basically a fight over her song but in this fight she's not limited to the immediate tools of her trade, her most valuable weapons, rather there are other means available here and it's for this reason I believe that this, perhaps, is the line that her reasoning takes that she's quite able to use means that are really ugly. So, for example, there's this rumor going around that Josephine intends upon shortening her coloratura... Now, I've never even noticed any coloratura in her singing and in general the voices of our folk tend toward being rough and untamed; our nature probably precludes any training that would allow for such refinement, but now Josephine is threatening to shorten her coloratura, not that they'd be eliminated entirely, just shortened. It's quite likely that she's followed through on this though I can't say that I've noticed any particular differences in the way that she sings versus how it used to be. Our folk as a whole has continued on listening just as we listened earlier, there haven't been any comments made as regards the coloratura and we haven't altered our stance in the least as regards her petition indeed, nothing seems to have changed. Just as Josephine has always been so charming in her bearing (Gestalt), so too there's no denying it her thinking is also, often enough, quite charming. Thus, for instance, after one of her performances with the abbreviated coloratura as if her resolution, really, had been all too hard on us so she announced that next time around she'd resume doing her full repertoire, a full blown concert with all of the extras. But, then again, right after the next concert she changed her mind once again and declared that from here on out there wouldn't be any coloratura at all and that this was her final, irrevocable decision and, moreover, she didn't even want to discuss the matter any further. Now, the folk listened along to all of these clarifications, decisions and counter decisions just like it always pays attention to the tantrums of a young child: we all wished for the best outcome but none of this seemed to have any connection to reality.

But Josephine wouldn't let up. Next thing you know she's claiming to have injured her foot whilst working and this injury would make it extremely difficult for her to stand during her performances and, since it was necessary for her to sing standing up, well, so now she doesn't have any other choice other than shortening her concerts. Despite the circumstance that she'd now come limping to center stage and that she allowed her entourage to help her along, despite all of this there wasn't a single one of us who believed that she had really hurt herself. Although we're all quite willing to admit that Josephine is a bit more sensitive than the rest of us, all the same as a folk we're very well known for being exceptional in our industriousness, we're hard workers one and all and Josephine, no matter what she says, Josephine is one of us. If everyone were to start limping about every time he would scrape up his knee, well, we'd all be limping about constantly.

Now, whether or not she allows herself to be led about by her admirers and no matter how often she appears before us in such a piteous manner, we don't let any of this have the least effect on how much we admire her performances, we go on listening to her singing exactly the same as always, with thankfulness and rapture, and we don't make a big deal out of the length or brevity of her performance.

Since she's not able to go on limping forever she discovers something else: sometimes she claims exhaustion, sometimes she says that she's "not in voice," and sometimes she claims that she's just too weak. Besides her singing we now get to enjoy these theatrics! We take note of how her admiring entourage is encouraging her backstage, they're all pleading with her and practically down on their knees begging her to step forward and sing. She says that she'd really like to do so but she can't. They all do their best to console her, they do everything possible to flatter her, they practically pick her up and carry her forward to the spot where she's known to appear, the spot where she's wont to perform and it's there that the crowd has gathered. Finally, and amidst an inexplicable outbreak of tears, finally she gives in, but then despite her best intentions and just as she's about to start into her song limp, her arms hanging down at her sides, not splayed out as they typically would be but rather hanging down as if they were dead appendages, and upon seeing them one easily gets the impression that somehow they've shrunk and just then as she's drawing in her first breath... it's obvious that she can't manage, her head jerks to one side and in the last moment she crumbles before us. But then at the very last moment, indeed, she's managed to pull herself together again and she's singing... I don't believe that it sounds any different than the usual, perhaps if one has an ear for distinguishing such subtleties, perhaps one might hear a bit more enthusiasm, a little more excitement that blends in quite well. And then, after she's finished she's a good deal less tired than when she began, it's with a firm step that she distances herself from us that is if you call the way she pitter-patters about as possibly having any firmness she turns down all the assistance that is being offered her by her contingent; it's with a cold stare that she testily examines the crowd that respectfully draws itself back, making way for her exit.

That's how her last performance ended but the most recent news is that her gala encore has fallen through totally, she didn't even show her face, she's disappeared entirely. Not only are her admirers out searching for her, there's a goodly number of us who are out looking for her too it's all for naught, she's disappeared entirely, she won't sign any more, she won't even allow us so much as to beg her for a performance, she's left us completely in the lurch.

It's odd how poorly her reasoning functions, this clever artiste, how mistaken and how contradictory; one would have to believe that she doesn't reason at all, that rather she's merely being driven on by her destiny a destiny that amongst us can only forebode ill. She has removed herself from practicing her art, she herself has destroyed the power that enabled her to take charge over our inner being. How could she ever have attained this ability seeing as how she understands so little about us, the depths of our soul. She's hidden herself away and won't sing; but our folk, ever calm, without showing the slightest sign of disturbance, practically in the guise of the master a mass that is at one with itself and essentially an entity that despite all appearances to the contrary is one that can only give gifts to others but is never able to receive any, not even from the likes of Josephine our folk continues along its path.

As regards Josephine there's no hope left, her time is over and I'm already able to see the last word regarding her existence, the last dying whistle of her tune as it fades into silence. She's merely a small episode in the never ending saga of our folk, a bit of history, and we'll be able to rise above our loss, our folk shall continue on. But then, it won't be that easy how are we to assemble together in total silence? Indeed, we weren't all that silent even when she was with us, was her actual whistling louder and more lively than our memory of it, am I saying anything in posing such a riddle? And was it ever anything more than a memory even when she still lived, rather isn't it much more the case that our folk in its wisdom, our folk rated her song so highly even due to this, because it was something that bespoke what is immortal, something that we'd never lose. Perhaps then, indeed, we won't be missing her all that much.

But Josephine, Josephine who has now been released from all of our earthly travails that, in her opinion, lie in wait for anyone who has been chosen to rise above the mundane it is with joy that she shall become lost in the countless multitude who make up our heroes, the heroes of our folk; and soon, seeing as how we're such awful historians, soon in a heightened state of blissful release (gesteigerte Erlösung) she too shall be forgotten along with all of her brothers and sisters, there is so much that we tend to forget...

Story 17

THE GREAT WALL OF CHINA

The Great Wall of China was finished at its northernmost location. The construction work moved up from the south-east and south-west and joined at this point. The system of building in sections was also followed on a small scale within the two great armies of workers, the eastern and western. It was carried out in the following manner: groups of about twenty workers were formed, each of which had to take on a section of the wall, about five hundred metres. A neighbouring group then built a wall of similar length to meet it. But afterwards, when the sections were fully joined, construction was not continued on any further at the end of this thousand metre section. Instead the groups of workers were shipped off again to build the wall in completely different regions. Naturally, with this method many large gaps arose, which were filled in only gradually and slowly, many of them not until after it had already been reported that the building of the wall was complete.

In fact, there are said to be gaps which have never been built in at all, although that's merely an assertion which probably belongs among the many legends which have arisen about the structure and which, for individual people at least, are impossible to prove with their own eyes and according to their own standards, because the structure is so immense.

Now, at first one might think it would have been more advantageous in every way to build in continuous sections or at least continuously within two main sections. For the wall was conceived as a protection against the people of the north, as was commonly announced and universally known. But how can protection be provided by a wall which is not built continuously? In fact, not only can such a wall not protect, but the structure itself is in constant danger. Those parts of the wall left standing abandoned in particular regions could easily be destroyed again and again by the nomads, especially by those back then who, worried about the building of the wall, changed their place of residence with incredible speed, like grasshoppers, and thus perhaps had an even better overall view of how the construction was proceeding than we did, the people who built it.

However, there was no other way to carry out the construction except the way it happened. In order to understand this, one must consider the following: the wall was to be a protection for centuries; thus, the essential prerequisites for the work were the most careful construction, the use of the architectural wisdom of all known ages and peoples, and an enduring sense of personal responsibility in the builders. Of course, for the more humble tasks one could use ignorant day labourers from the people—the men, women, and children who offered their services for good money.

But the supervision of even four day labourers required a knowledgeable man, an educated expert in construction, someone who was capable of feeling sympathy deep in his heart for what was at stake here. And the higher the challenge, the greater the demands. And such men were in fact available—if not the crowds of them which this construction could have used, at least in great numbers.

They did not set about this task recklessly. Fifty years before the start of construction it was announced throughout the whole region of China which was to be enclosed within the wall that architecture and especially masonry were the most important areas of knowledge, and everything else was recognized only to the extent that it had some relationship to those. I still remember very well how as small children who could hardly walk we stood in our teacher's little garden and had to construct a sort of wall out of pebbles, and how the teacher gathered up his coat and ran against the wall, naturally making everything collapse, and then scolded us so much for the weakness of our construction that we ran off in all directions howling to our parents. A tiny incident, but an indication of the spirit of the times.

I was lucky that at twenty years of age, when I passed the final examination of the lowest school, the construction of the wall was just starting. I say lucky because many who earlier had attained the highest limit of education available to them for years had no idea what to do with their knowledge and wandered around uselessly, with the most splendid architectural plans in their heads, and a great many of them just went downhill from there. But the ones who finally got to work as supervisors on the construction, even if they had the lowest rank, were really worthy of their position. They were masons who had given much thought to the construction and never stopped thinking about it, men who, right from the first stone which they sunk into the ground, had a sense of themselves as part of the wall. Such masons, of course, were driven not only by the desire to carry out the work as thoroughly as possible but also by impatience to see the structure standing there in its complete final perfection. Day labourers do not experience this impatience. They are driven only by their pay. The higher supervisors and, indeed, even the middle supervisors, see enough from their various perspectives on the growth of the wall to keep their spirits energized. But the subordinate supervisors, men who were mentally far above their small, more trivial tasks, had to be catered to in other ways. One could not, for example, let them lay one building block on top of another in an uninhabited region of the mountains, hundreds of miles from their homes, for months or even years at a time. The hopelessness of such a hard task, which could not be completed even in a long human lifetime, would have caused them distress and, more than anything else, made them worthless for work. For that reason they chose the system of building in sections.

Five hundred metres could be completed in something like five years, by which time naturally the supervisors were as a rule too exhausted and had lost all faith in themselves, in the building, and in the world.

Thus, while they were still experiencing the elation of the celebrations for the joining up of a thousand metres of the wall, they were shipped far, far away. On their journey they saw here and there finished sections of the wall rising up; they passed through the quarters of the higher administrators, who gave them gifts as badges of honour, and they heard the rejoicing of new armies of workers streaming past them out of the depths of the land, saw forests being laid low, wood designated as scaffolding for the wall, witnessed mountains being broken up into rocks for the wall, and heard in the holy places the hymns of the pious praying for the construction to be finished. All this calmed their impatience. The quiet life of home, where they spent some time, reinvigorated them. The high regard which all those doing the building enjoyed, the devout humility with which people listened to their reports, the trust that simple quiet citizens had that the wall would be completed someday—all this tuned the strings of their souls. Then, like eternally hopeful children, they took leave of their home. The enthusiasm for labouring once again at the people's work became irresistible. They set out from their houses earlier than necessary, and half the village accompanied them for a long way. On all the roads there were groups of people, pennants, banners—they had never seen how great and rich and beautiful and endearing their country was. Every countryman was a brother for whom they were building a protective wall and who would thank him with everything he had and was for all his life. Unity! Unity! Shoulder to shoulder, a coordinated movement of the people, their blood no longer confined in the limited circulation of the body but rolling sweetly and yet still returning through the infinite extent of China.

In view of all this, the system of piecemeal building becomes understandable. But there were still other reasons, too. And there is nothing strange in the fact that I have held off on this point for so long. It is the central issue in the whole construction of the wall, no matter how unimportant it appears at first. If I want to convey the ideas and experiences of that time and make them intelligible, I cannot probe deeply enough into this particular question.

First, one must realize that at that time certain achievements were brought to fruition which rank only slightly behind the Tower of Babel, although in the pleasure they gave to God, at least by human reckoning, they made an impression exactly the opposite of that structure. I mention this because at the time construction was beginning a scholar wrote a book in which he drew this comparison very precisely.

In it he tried to show that the Tower of Babel had failed to attain its goal not for the reasons commonly asserted, or at least that the most important cause was not among these well known ones. He not only based his proofs on texts and reports, but also claimed to have carried out personal inspections of the location and thus to have found that the structure collapsed and had to collapse because of the weakness of its foundation. And it is true that in this respect our age was far superior to that one long ago. Almost every educated person in our age was a mason by profession and infallible when it came to the business of laying foundations.

But it was not at all the scholar's aim to prove this. He claimed that the great wall alone would for the first time in the age of human beings create a secure foundation for a new Tower of Babel. So first the wall and then the tower. In those days the book was in everyone's hands, but I confess that even today I do not understand exactly how he imagined this tower. How could the wall, which never once took the form of a circle but only a sort of quarter or half circle, provide the foundation for a tower? But it could be meant only in a spiritual sense. But then why the wall, which was still something real, a product of the efforts and lives of hundreds of thousands of people? And why were there plans in the book—admittedly hazy plans—sketching the tower, as well as detailed proposals about how the energies of the people could be channelled into powerfully new work.

There was a great deal of mental confusion at the time—his book is only one example—perhaps simply because so many people were trying as hard as they could to join together for a single purpose. Human nature, which is fundamentally careless and by nature like the whirling dust, endures no restraint. If it restricts itself, it will soon begin to shake the restraints madly and tear up walls, chains, and even itself all over the place.

It is possible that even these considerations, which argued against building the wall in the first place, were not ignored by the leadership when they decided on piecemeal construction. We—and here I'm really speaking on behalf of many—actually first found out about it by spelling out the orders from the highest levels of management and learned for ourselves that without the leadership neither our school learning nor our human understanding would have been adequate for the small position we had within the enormous totality.

In the office of the leadership—where it was and who sat there no one I asked knows or knew—in this office I imagine that all human thoughts and wishes revolve in a circle, and all human aims and fulfilments in a circle going in the opposite direction. And through the window the reflection of the divine worlds fell onto the hands of the leadership as they drew up the plans.

And for this reason the incorruptible observer will reject the notion that if the leadership had seriously wanted a continuous construction of the wall, they would not have been able to overcome the difficulties standing in the way. So the only conclusion left is that the leadership deliberately chose piecemeal construction. But building in sections was something merely makeshift and impractical. So the conclusion remains that the leadership wanted something impractical. An odd conclusion! True enough, and yet from another perspective it had some inherent justification.

Nowadays one can perhaps speak about it without danger. At that time for many people, even the best, there was a secret principle: Try with all your powers to understand the orders of the leadership, but only up to a certain limit—then stop thinking about them. A very reasonable principle, which incidentally found an even wider interpretation in a later often repeated comparison: Stop further thinking about it, not because it could harm you—it is not at all certain that it will harm you. In this matter one cannot speak in general about harming or not harming. What will happen to you is like a river in spring. It rises, grows stronger, eats away powerfully at the land along its shores, and still maintains its own course down into the sea and is more welcome as a fitter partner for the sea. Reflect upon the orders of the leadership as far as that. But then the river overflows its banks, loses its form and shape, slows down its forward movement, tries, contrary to its destiny, to form small seas inland, damages the fields, and yet cannot maintain its expansion long, but runs back within its banks, in fact, even dries up miserably in the hot time of year which follows. Do not reflect on the orders of the leadership to that extent.

Now, this comparison may perhaps have been extraordinarily apt during the construction of the wall, but it has at most only a limited relevance to my present report. For my investigation is only historical. There is no lightning strike flashing any more from storm clouds which have long since vanished, and thus I may seek an explanation for the piecemeal construction which goes further than the one people were satisfied with back then. The limits which my ability to think sets for me are certainly narrow enough, but the region one would have to pass through here is endless.

Against whom was the great wall to provide protection? Against the people of the north. I come from south-east China. No northern people can threaten us there. We read about them in the books of the ancients. The atrocities which their nature prompts them to commit make us heave a sigh on our peaceful porches. In the faithfully accurate pictures of artists we see the faces of this damnation, with their mouths flung open, the sharp pointed teeth stuck in their jaws, their straining eyes, which seem to be squinting for someone to seize, whom their jaws will crush and rip to pieces. When children are naughty, we hold up these pictures in front of them, and they immediately burst into tears and run into our arms.

But we know nothing else about these northern lands. We have never seen them, and if we remain in our village, we never will see them, even if they charge straight at us and hunt us on their wild horses. The land is so huge, it would not permit them to reach us, and they would lose themselves in empty air.

So if things are like this, why do we leave our homes, the river and bridges, our mothers and fathers, our crying wives, our children in need of education, and go to school in the distant city, with our thoughts on the wall to the north, even further away? Why? Ask the leadership. They know us. As they mull over their immense concerns, they know about us, understand our small worries, see us all sitting together in our humble huts, and approve or disapprove of the prayer which the father of the house says in the evening surrounded by his family. And if I may be permitted such ideas about the leadership, then I must say that in my view the leadership existed even earlier. It did not come together like some high mandarins hastily summoned to a meeting by a beautiful dream of the future, something hastily concluded, a meeting which saw to it that the general population was driven from their beds by a knocking on the door so that they could carry out the decision, even if it was only to set up an lantern in honour of a god who had shown favour to the masters the day before, so that he could thrash them in some dark corner the next day, when the lantern had only just died out. On the contrary, I imagine the leadership has always existed, along with the decision to construct the wall as well. Innocent northern people believed they were the cause; the admirable innocent emperor believed he had given orders for it. We who were builders of the wall know otherwise and are silent.

Even during the construction of the wall and afterwards, right up to the present day, I have devoted myself almost exclusively to the histories of different people. There are certain questions for which one can, to some extent, get to the heart of the matter only in this way. Using this method I have found that we Chinese possess certain popular and state institutions which are uniquely clear and, then again, others which are uniquely obscure. Tracking down the reasons for these, especially for the latter phenomena, always appealed to me, and still does, and the construction of the wall is fundamentally concerned with these issues.

Now, among our most obscure institutions one can certainly include the empire itself. Of course, in Peking, right in the court, there is some clarity about it, although even this is more apparent than real. And the teachers of constitutional law and history in the schools of higher learning give out that they are precisely informed about these things and that they are able to pass this knowledge on to their students.

The deeper one descends into the lower schools, understandably the more the doubts about the students' own knowledge disappear, and a superficial education surges up as high as a mountain around a few precepts drilled into them for centuries, sayings which, in fact, have lost nothing of their eternal truth, but which remain also eternally unrecognised in the mist and fog.

But, in my view, it's precisely the empire we should be asking the people about, because in them the empire has its final support. It's true that in this matter I can speak once again only about my own homeland. Other than the agricultural deities and the service to them, which so beautifully and variously fills up the entire year, our thinking concerns itself only with the emperor. But not with the present emperor. We'd rather think about the present one if we knew who he was or anything definite about him. We were naturally always trying—and it's the single curiosity which satisfies us—to find out something or other about him, but, no matter how strange this sounds, it was hardly possible to learn anything, either from pilgrims, even though they wandered through much of our land, or from the close or remote villages, or from boatmen, although they have travelled not merely on our little waterways but also on the sacred rivers. True, we heard a great deal, but could gather nothing from the many details.

Our land is so huge, that no fairy tale can adequately deal with its size. Heaven hardly covers it all. And Peking is only a point, the imperial palace only a tiny dot. It's true that, by contrast, throughout all the different levels of the world the emperor, as emperor, is great. But the living emperor, a man like us, lies on a peaceful bed, just as we do. It is, no doubt, of ample proportions, but it could be merely narrow and short. Like us, he sometime stretches out his limbs and, if he is very tired, yawns with his delicately delineated mouth. But how are we to know about that thousands of miles to the south, where we almost border on the Tibetan highlands? Besides, any report which came, even if it reached us, would get there much too late and would be long out of date. Around the emperor the glittering and yet mysterious court throngs—malice and enmity clothed as servants and friends, the counterbalance to the imperial power, with their poisoned arrows always trying to shoot the emperor down from his side of the balance scales. The empire is immortal, but the individual emperor falls and collapses. Even entire dynasties finally sink down and breathe their one last death rattle. The people will never know anything about these struggles and sufferings. Like those who have come too late, like strangers to the city, they stand at the end of the thickly populated side alleyways, quietly living off the provisions they have brought with them, while far off in the market place right in the middle foreground the execution of their master is taking place.

There is a legend which expresses this relationship well.

The Emperor—so they say—has sent a message, directly from his death bed, to you alone, his pathetic subject, a tiny shadow which has taken refuge at the furthest distance from the imperial sun. He ordered the herald to kneel down beside his bed and whispered the message into his ear. He thought it was so important that he had the herald repeat it back to him. He confirmed the accuracy of the verbal message by nodding his head. And in front of the entire crowd of those who've come to witness his death—all the obstructing walls have been broken down and all the great ones of his empire are standing in a circle on the broad and high soaring flights of stairs—in front of all of them he dispatched his herald. The messenger started off at once, a powerful, tireless man. Sticking one arm out and then another, he makes his way through the crowd. If he runs into resistance, he points to his breast where there is a sign of the sun. So he moves forward easily, unlike anyone else. But the crowd is so huge; its dwelling places are infinite. If there were an open field, how he would fly along, and soon you would hear the marvellous pounding of his fist on your door. But instead of that, how futile are all his efforts. He is still forcing his way through the private rooms of the innermost palace. He will never he win his way through. And if he did manage that, nothing would have been achieved. He would have to fight his way down the steps, and, if he managed to do that, nothing would have been achieved. He would have to stride through the courtyards, and after the courtyards the second palace encircling the first, and, then again, stairs and courtyards, and then, once again, a palace, and so on for thousands of years. And if he finally did burst through the outermost door—but that can never, never happen—the royal capital city, the centre of the world, is still there in front of him, piled high and full of sediment. No one pushes his way through here, certainly not with a message from a dead man. But you sit at your window and dream of that message when evening comes.

That's exactly how our people look at the emperor, hopelessly and full of hope. They don't know which emperor is on the throne, and there are even doubts about the name of the dynasty. In the schools they learn a great deal about things like the succession, but the common uncertainty in this respect is so great that even the best pupils are drawn into it. In our villages emperors long since dead are set on the throne, and one of them who still lives on only in songs had one of his announcements issued a little while ago, which the priest read out from the altar. Battles from our most ancient history are now fought for the first time, and with a glowing face your neighbour charges into your house with the report. The imperial wives, over indulged on silk cushions, alienated from noble customs by shrewd courtiers, swollen with thirst for power, driven by greed, excessive in their lust, are always committing their evil acts over again.

The further back they are in time, the more terrible all their colours glow, and with a loud cry of grief our village eventually gets to learn how an empress thousands of years ago drank her husband's blood in lengthy gulps.

That, then, is how the people deal with the rulers from the past, but they mix up the present rulers with the dead ones. If once, once in a person's lifetime an imperial official travelling around the province comes into our village, sets out some demands or other in the name of the rulers, checks the tax lists, attends a school class, interrogates the priest about our comings and goings, and then, before climbing into his sedan chair, summarizes everything in a long sermon to the assembled local population, at that point a smile crosses every face, one man looks furtively at another and bends over his children, so as not to let the official see him. How, people think, can he speak of a dead man as if he were alive. This emperor already died a long time ago, the dynasty has been extinguished, the official is having fun with us. But we'll act as if we didn't notice, so that we don't hurt his feelings. However, in all seriousness we'll obey only our present ruler, for anything else would be a sin. And behind the official's sedan chair as it hurries away their arises from the already decomposed urn someone or other arbitrarily endorsed as ruler of the village.

Similarly, with us people are, as a rule, little affected by political revolutions and contemporary wars. Here I recall an incident from my youth. In a neighbouring but still very far distant province a rebellion broke out. I cannot remember the causes any more. Besides, they are not important here. In that province reasons for rebellion arise every new day—they are an excitable people. Well, on one occasion a rebel pamphlet was brought to my father's house by a beggar who had travelled through that province. It happened to be a holiday. Our living room was full of guests. The priest sat in their midst and studied the pamphlet. Suddenly everyone started laughing, the sheet was torn to pieces in the general confusion, and the beggar was chased out of the room with blows, although he had already been richly rewarded. Everyone scattered and ran out into the beautiful day. Why? The dialect of the neighbouring province is essentially different from ours, and these differences manifest themselves also in certain forms of the written language, which for us have an antiquated character. Well, the priest had scarcely read two pages like that, and people had already decided. Old matters heard long ago, and long since got over. And although—as I recall from my memory—a horrifying way of life seemed to speak irrefutably through the beggar, people laughed and shook their head and were unwilling to hear any more. That's how ready people are among us to obliterate the present.

If one wanted to conclude from such phenomena that we basically have no emperor at all, one would not be far from the truth. I need to say it again and again: There is perhaps no people more faithful to the emperor than we are in the south, but the emperor derives no benefits from our loyalty. It's true that on the way out of our village there stands on a little pillar the sacred dragon, which, for as long as men can remember, has paid tribute by blowing its fiery breath straight in the direction of Peking. But for the people in the village Peking itself is much stranger than living in the next world. Could there really be a village where houses stand right beside each other covering the fields and reaching further than the view from our hills, with men standing shoulder to shoulder between these houses day and night? Rather than imagining such a city, it's easier for us to believe that Peking and its emperor are one, something like a cloud, peacefully moving along under the sun as the ages pass.

Now, the consequence of such opinions is a life which is to some extent free and uncontrolled. Not in any way immoral—purity of morals like those in my homeland I have hardly ever come across in my travels. But nonetheless a life that stands under no present laws and only pays attention to the wisdom and advice which reach across to us from ancient times.

I guard again generalizations and do not claim that things like this go on in all ten thousand villages of our province or, indeed, in all five hundred provinces of China. But on the basis of the many writings which I have read concerning this subject, as well as on the basis of my many observations, especially since the construction of the wall with its human material provided an opportunity for a man of feeling to travel through the souls of almost all the provinces—on the basis of all this perhaps I may truly state that with respect to the emperor the prevailing idea again and again reveals a certain universal essential feature common to the conception in my homeland. Now, I have no desire at all to let this conception stand as a virtue—quite the contrary. It's true that in the main things the blame rests with the government, which in the oldest empire on earth right up to the present day has not been able or has, among other things, neglected to cultivate the institution of empire sufficiently clearly so that it is immediately and ceaselessly effective right up to the most remote frontiers of the empire. On the other hand, however, there is in this also a weakness in the people's power of imagining or believing, which has not succeeded in pulling the empire out of its deep contemplative state in Peking and making it something fully vital and present in the hearts of subjects, who nonetheless want nothing better than to feel its touch once and then die from the experience.

So this conception is really not a virtue. It's all the more striking that this very weakness appears to be one of the most important ways of unifying our people.

Indeed, if one may go so far as to use the expression, it is the very ground itself on which we live. To provide a detailed account of why we have a flaw here would amount not just to rattling our consciences but, what is much more serious, to making our feet tremble. And therefore I do not wish to go any further in the investigation of these questions at the present time.

Story 18

UP IN THE GALLERY

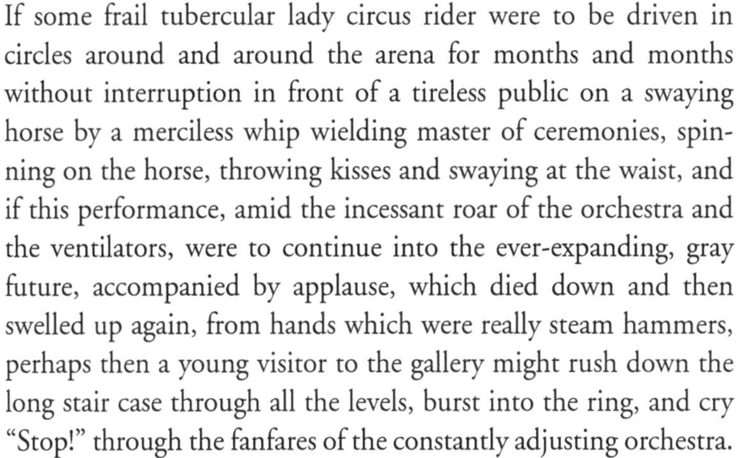

If some frail tubercular lady circus rider were to be driven in circles around and around the arena for months and months without interruption in front of a tireless public on a swaying horse by a merciless whip wielding master of ceremonies, spinning on the horse, throwing kisses and swaying at the waist, and if this performance, amid the incessant roar of the orchestra and the ventilators, were to continue into the ever-expanding, gray future, accompanied by applause, which died down and then swelled up again, from hands which were really steam hammers, perhaps then a young visitor to the gallery might rush down the long stair case through all the levels, burst into the ring, and cry "Stop!" through the fanfares of the constantly adjusting orchestra.

But since things are not like that—since a beautiful woman, in white and red, flies in through curtains which proud men in livery open in front of her, since the director, devotedly seeking her eyes, breathes in her direction, behaving like an animal, and, as a precaution, lifts her up on the dapple-gray horse, as if she were his grand-daughter, the one he loved more than anything else, as she starts a dangerous journey, but he cannot decide to give the signal with his whip and finally, controlling himself, gives it a crack, runs right beside the horse with his mouth open, follows the rider's leaps with a sharp gaze, hardly capable of comprehending her skill, tries to warn her by calling out in English, furiously castigating the grooms holding hoops, telling them to pay the most scrupulous attention, and begs the orchestra, with upraised arms, to be quiet before the great jump, finally lifts the small woman down from the trembling horse, kisses her on both cheeks, considers no public tribute adequate, while she herself, leaning on him, high on the tips of her toes, with dust swirling around her, arms outstretched and head thrown back, wants to share her luck with the entire circus—since this is how things are, the visitor to the gallery puts his face on the railing and, sinking into the final march as if into a difficult dream, weeps, without realizing it.

Story 19

ABSENT-MINDED WINDOW-GAZING

What are we to do with these spring days that are now fast coming on? Early this morning the sky was gray, but if you go to the window now you are surprised and lean your cheek against the latch of the casement.

The sun is already setting, but down below you see it lighting up the face of the little girl who strolls along looking about her, and at the same time you see her eclipsed by the shadow of the man behind overtaking her.

And then the man has passed by and the little girl's face is quite bright.

Story 20

CLOTHES

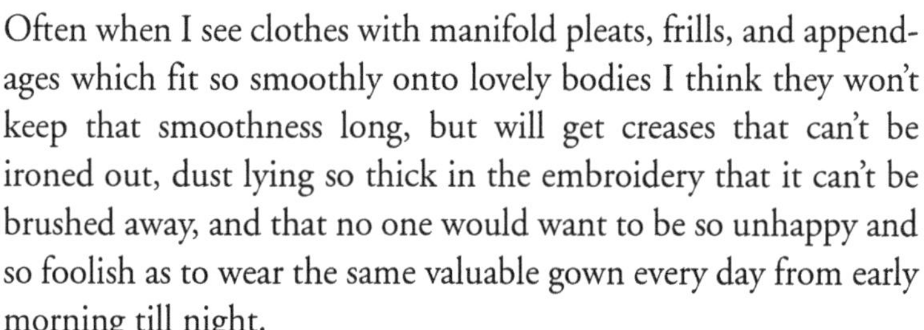

Often when I see clothes with manifold pleats, frills, and appendages which fit so smoothly onto lovely bodies I think they won't keep that smoothness long, but will get creases that can't be ironed out, dust lying so thick in the embroidery that it can't be brushed away, and that no one would want to be so unhappy and so foolish as to wear the same valuable gown every day from early morning till night.

And yet I see girls who are lovely enough and display attractive muscles and small bones and smooth skin and masses of delicate hair, and nonetheless appear day in, day out, in this same natural fancy dress, always propping the same face on the same palms and letting it be reflected from the looking glass.

Only sometimes at night, on coming home late from a party, it seems in the looking glass to be worn out, puffy, dusty, already seen by too many people, and hardly wearable any longer.

Story 21

THE TRADESMAN

It is possible that some people are sorry for me, but I am not aware of it. My small business fills me with worries that make my forehead and temples ache inside yet without giving any prospect of relief, for my business is a small business.

I have to spend hours beforehand making things ready, jogging the caretaker's memory, warning him about mistakes he is likely to commit, and puzzling out in one season of the year what the next season's fashions are to be, not such as are followed by the people I know but those that will appeal to inaccessible peasants in the depths of the country.

My money is in the hands of strangers; the state of their affairs must be a mystery to me; the ill luck that might overwhelm them I cannot foresee; how could I possibly avert it! Perhaps they are running into extravagance and giving a banquet in some inn garden, some of them may be attending the banquet as a brief respite before their flight to America.

When at the close of a working day I turn the key on my business and suddenly see before me hours in which I shall be able to do nothing to satisfy its never ending demands, then the excitement which I drove far away from me in the morning comes back like a returning tide, but cannot be contained in me and sweeps me aimlessly away with it.

And yet I can make no use of this impulse, I can only go home, for my face and hands are dirty and sweaty, my clothes are stained and dusty, my working cap is on my head, and my shoes are scratched with the nails of crates. I go home as if lifted on a wave, snapping the fingers of both hands, and caress the hair of any children I meet.

But the way is short. Soon I reach my house, open the door of the lift, and step in.

I see that now, of a sudden, I am alone. Others who have to climb stairways tire a little as they climb, have to wait with quick panting breath till someone opens the door of the flat, which gives them an excuse for being irritable and impatient, have to traverse the hallway where hats are hung up, and not until they go down a lobby past several glass doors and come into their own room are they alone.

But I am alone in the lift, immediately, and on my knees gaze into the narrow looking glass. As the lift begins to rise, I say: 'Quiet now, back with you, is it the shadow of the trees you want to make for, or behind the window curtains, or into the garden arbor?'

I say that behind my teeth, and the staircase flows down past the opaque glass panes like running water.

'Fly then; let your wings, which I have never seen, carry you into the village hollow or as far as Paris, if that's where you want to go.

'But enjoy yourselves there looking out of the window, see the processions converging out of three streets at once, not giving way to each other but marching through each other and leaving the open space free again as their last ranks draw off. Wave your handkerchiefs, be indignant, be moved, acclaim the beautiful lady who drives past.

'Cross over the stream on the wooden bridge, nod to the children bathing and gape at the Hurrah! Rising from the thousand sailors on the distant battleship.

'Follow the trail of the inconspicuous little man, and when you have pushed him into a doorway, rob him, and then watch him, each with your hands in your pockets, as he sadly goes his way along the left hand street.

'The police dispersed on galloping horses rein in their mounts and thrust you back. Let them, the empty streets will dishearten them, I know. What did I tell you, they are riding away already in couples, slowly around the corners, at full speed across the squares.'

Then I have to leave the lift, send it down again, and ring the bell, and the maid opens the door while I say: Good evening.

OTHER BOOKS YOU MAY LIKE

- 12 Years a Slave by Solomon Northup, ISBN: 9789390492374
- 51 Most Powerful Prayers by Ryan, ISBN: 9789354990847
- A Christmas Carol by Charles Dickens, ISBN: 9788193545874
- A Cloud by Day, a Fire by Night by AW Tozer, ISBN: 9789354990854
- A Streetcar Named Desire by Tennessee Williams, ISBN: 9788194748601
- Abraham Lincoln by Lord Charnwood, ISBN: 9789380914251
- Absolute Surrender by Andrew Murray, ISBN: 9789389716269
- Annihilation of Caste by Dr B.R. Ambedkar, ISBN: 9789390492732
- Awakened Imagination by Neville Goddard, ISBN: 9789389157086
- Be What You Wish by Neville Goddard, ISBN: 9789387669550
- Believe in Yourself by Joseph Murphy, ISBN: 9789388118385
- Chanakya Neeti by Chanakya, ISBN: 9789389716276
- Civilization and Its Discontents by Sigmund Freud, ISBN: 9789387669499
- Delighting in God by AW Tozer, ISBN: 9788194748632
- Experiencing the Holy Spirit by Andrew Murray, ISBN: 9788194764809
- Feeling is the Secret by Neville Goddard, ISBN: 9789389157109
- George Orwell Combo : Animal Farm & 1984, ISBN: 9789390492459
- Gravity by George Gamow, ISBN: 9789388118484
- Guerrilla Warfare by Ernesto Che Guevara, ISBN: 9789354990366
- How I Made $2 Million in the Stock Market by N. Darvas, ISBN: 9789389716283
- How to Attract Money by Joseph Murphy, ISBN: 9789388118408
- How to be filled with the Holy Spirit by AW Tozer, ISBN: 9789389157116
- How to Develop Self Confidence by Dale Carnegie, ISBN: 9789387669000
- How to Enjoy Your Life and Your Job by Dale Carnegie, ISBN: 9789387669017
- How to Stop Worrying and Start Living by Dale Carnegie, ISBN: 9789380914817
- How to Win Friends and Influence People by D. Carnegie, ISBN: 9788180320217

OTHER BOOKS YOU MAY LIKE

- In His Steps by Charles M. Sheldon, ISBN: 9789390492794
- Jail Diary and Other Writings by Bhagat Singh, ISBN: 9789390492398
- Know Your Worth by NK Sondhi & Vibha Malhotra, ISBN: 9788180320231
- Life of Christ by Fulton J. Sheen, ISBN: 9789389716306
- Man: The Dwelling Place of God by AW Tozer, ISBN: 9789354990656
- Maneaters of Kumaon by Jim Corbett, ISBN: 9789354990731
- Mansarover 2 (Hindi) by Premchand, ISBN: 9789380914985
- Meditation and Its Methods by Swami Vivekananda, ISBN: 9789389716320
- Meditations by Marcus Aurelius, ISBN: 9789388118736
- My Experiments with Truth by Mahatma Gandhi, ISBN: 9789387669291
- My Inventions: The Autobiography of Nikola Tesla, ISBN: 9789388118132
- Paths to Power by AW Tozer, ISBN: Forthcoming
- Relativity by Albert Einstein, ISBN: 9789380914220
- Reminiscences of a Stock Operator by Edwin Lefevre, ISBN: 9788194764816
- Scientific Healing Affirmations by P. Yogananda, ISBN: 9789389716344
- Selected Stories of Rabindranath Tagore by Tagore, ISBN: 9789380914770
- Student's Encyclopedia of G. K. by GP Editors, ISBN: 9789380914190
- Success Through a Positive Mental Attitude by N. Hill, ISBN: 9789390492435
- The Alchemy of Happiness by Al-Ghazzali, ISBN: 9789387669505
- The Art of War by Sun Tzu, ISBN: 9789380914893
- The Autobiography of a Yogi by Paramahansa Yogananda, ISBN: 9789380914602
- The Book of Enoch by Enoch, ISBN: 9789390492480
- The Diary of a Young Girl by Anne Frank, ISBN: 9789380914312
- The Dynamic Laws of Prosperity by Catherine Ponder, ISBN: 9789388118156
- The Elements of Style by William Strunk, ISBN: 9789389157123
- The Game of Life and How to Play It by Florence Shinn, ISBN: 9789387669390

Develop your reading habit | **Gift books to your friends**

OTHER BOOKS YOU MAY LIKE

- The Imitation of Christ by Thomas À Kempis, ISBN: 9789388118057
- The Knowledge of the Holy by AW Tozer, ISBN: 9789389157130
- The Law by Neville Goddard, ISBN: 9789390492886
- The Law of Success by Napoleon Hill, ISBN: 9788180320927
- The Light of Asia by Sir Edwin Arnold, ISBN: 9789380914923
- The Magic of Believing by Claudie Bristol, ISBN: 9789388118149
- The Magic of Faith by Joseph Murphy, ISBN: 9789388118743
- The Miracles of Your Mind by Joseph Murphy, ISBN: 9788180320743
- The Origin of Species by Charles Darwin, ISBN: 9788180320453
- The Power of Awareness by Neville Goddard, ISBN: 9789387669406
- The Power of Positive Thinking by Norman Vincent Peale, ISBN: 9789388118569
- The Power of Your Subconscious Mind by Joseph Murphy, ISBN: 9788180320958
- The Problem of Increasing Human Energy by Nikola Tesla, ISBN: 9789354990953
- The Psychopathology of Everyday Life by Sigmund Freud, ISBN: 9789388118071
- The Pursuit of God by AW Tozer, ISBN: 9789389157147
- The Red Badge of Courage by Stephen Crane, ISBN: 9789354990977
- The Richest Man in Babylon by George S. Clason, ISBN: 9789387669369
- The Science of Getting Rich by Wallace D. Wattles, ISBN: 9788180320972
- The World as I See It by Albert Einstein, ISBN: 9789388118125
- The Yoga Sutras of Patanjali by Patanjali, ISBN: 9789389716351
- Think and Grow Rich by Napoleon Hill, ISBN: 9788180320255
- Thought Vibration by William Walker Atkinson, ISBN: 9789389157154
- Who were the Shudras by Dr B.R. Ambedkar, ISBN: 9789354991028
- Wuthering Heights by Emily Brontë, ISBN: 9788193545898
- Your Faith is Your Fortune by Neville Goddard, ISBN: 9789389157161
- Zen in the Art of Archery by Eugen Herrigel, ISBN: 9789354991059

Develop your reading habit | **Gift books to your friends**

www.ingramcontent.com/pod-product-compliance
Ingram Content Group UK Ltd.
Pitfield, Milton Keynes, MK11 3LW, UK
UKHW040007200726
13854UKWH00001B/89

9 789354 991103